QUANTUM
CONVENTION

QUANTUM CONVENTION

By Eric Schlich

2018 WINNER, KATHERINE ANNE PORTER PRIZE IN SHORT FICTION

University of North Texas Press
Denton, Texas

10 9 8 7 6 5 4 3 2 1

Permissions:
University of North Texas Press
1155 Union Circle #311336
Denton, Texas 76203-5017

∞The paper used in this book meets the minimum requirements of the American National
Standard for Permanence of Paper for Printed Library Materials, z39.48.1984. Binding
materials have been chosen for durability.

Library of Congress Cataloging-in-Publication Data

Names: Schlich, Eric, 1988– author.
Title: Quantum convention / by Eric Schlich.
Other titles: Katherine Anne Porter Prize in Short Fiction series no. 17.
Description: Denton, Texas : University of North Texas Press, [2018] |
    Series: Katherine Anne Porter Prize in Short Fiction ; Number 17 | "2018
    Winner, Katherine Anne Porter Prize in Short Fiction."
Identifiers: LCCN 2018029668| ISBN 9781574417364 (pbk. : alk. paper) | ISBN
    9781574417470 (ebook)
Subjects: | LCGFT: Magic realist fiction. | Short stories.
Classification: LCC PS3619.C427 A6 2018 | DDC 813/.6—dc23
LC record available at https://na01.safelinks.protection.outlook.com/?url=https%3A%2F%
2Flccn.loc.gov%2F2018029668&data=01%7C01%7Ckaren.devinney%40
unt.edu%7C17464ba096f64730003008d5e843ac1d%7C70de199207c
6480fa318a1afcba03983%7C0&sdata=B2FjMZewBv%2B1oJAZVT7u8Byft
XoWlk6bR2BZBPvUSZA%3D&reserved=0

Cover and text design by Rose Design

Quantum Convention is Number 17 in the Katherine Anne Porter Prize in Short
Fiction Series.

The electronic edition of this book was made possible by the support of the Vick Family
Foundation.

To Jade, and all her parallel selves.
For putting up with mine.

Contents

Acknowledgments   ix

Quantum Convention   1

The Keener   13

Not Nobody, Not Nohow   35

Lucidity   64

Night Thieves   86

Merlin Lives Next Door   109

Journal of a Cyclops   133

Lipless   151

Acknowledgments

I owe a debt to Aljean Harmetz's *The Making of the Wizard of Oz* (1977), from which I drew source material for "Not Nobody, Not Nohow."

My appreciation for the supporters of my writing is endless. I'm grateful to all:

Karen DeVinney, J. Andrew Briseño, Dolan Morgan, Bess Whitby, and Kimberly Bain for their work on the book and the Katherine Anne Porter series.

The editors of the publications where these stories previously appeared:

Crazyhorse: "Quantum Convention."

The Massachusetts Review: "Journal of a Cyclops."

Mississippi Review: "The Keener."

New South: "Lipless."

Nimrod: "Lucidity" and "Merlin Lives Next Door."

Redivider: "Night Thieves."

My fiction professors at Florida State: Elizabeth Stuckey-French and Mark Winegardner. Jennine Capó Crucet and my fellow writers in her debut short story collection class. My fiction professors at Bowling Green: Lawrence Coates, Michael Czyzniejewski, Wendell Mayo, and Josh Weil.

My fiction cohorts at FSU and BGSU.

Writer-friends Amy Mckenzie, Sam Holley, Anna Rose Welch, Kate Kimball, Amy Denham, C.J. Hauser, Jesse Goolsby, S.J. Sindu, and Anne Valente.

My family, without whom I might never have loved literature. Thank you for the wagon rides to the library, for always asking what I'm reading, and (of course) for the red shoes.

And Jade, my somebody.

Quantum Convention

In the Marriott ballroom a hundred of me have gathered. I thought it was going to feel like a funhouse—you know, with the mirrors—but it's nothing like a funhouse. It's more like a family reunion, except you don't know anyone and it's all cousins.

Fat Me is in the corner with a plate of kale chips. Every so often he shoots a glance at the spread of doughnuts, bagels, and cheese cubes. Across from him sits Mustache Me. (I'm tempted to say Pedophile Me. Jane's right. I can't pull off facial hair without looking like a creep.) Goatee Me—better, not great—is chatting with Fashion Disaster Me, who wears a neon orange jumpsuit. He's not the only one in an outfit. There's Prom Date Me in a tux, Hobo Me in a gray toboggan, and Drag Queen Me in a blonde wig.

"Hey! Sad Eyes!"

It takes a second to realize he means me. It's Mullet Me, waving me over to a table filled with more of me.

I say, "Hi. I'm Colin," and they all bust a gut. "Oh. Right. I guess you knew that."

"Hi, Colin. I'm Colin," says Suit Me.

"Oh! Wow. I'm Colin, too," says Aftershave Me.

"Guys, this is uncanny," says Sarcastic Me. "We really should get nametags."

"First time?" says Suit.

"Didn't mean to give myself away."

"We can always tell," says Mullet.

Then comes the expected opener: *What do you do?*

I think about bending the truth, saying I teach at a liberal arts college instead of a public high school, but I've never been a good liar. Maybe there's a me—Con Man Me?—who could give me a few pointers. I wait for the inevitable *Those who can't* joke, but it doesn't come. I guess I hate that joke in every uni.

"No shit," says Aftershave. "Me too. What subject?"

"English."

"Ouch," he says. "All those essays. Should have switched to math. Numbers, man. Practically teaches itself."

"Funny. That's what Mr. Farquad used to say."

"Hey!" the table cheers. "Fork point!"

A fork point, Mullet explains, is the moment one self splits into two. You know, like two roads diverge in the woods and all that. One self walks down one road, one walks the other. Except it's more like two roads and then two more roads and then two more . . . until you have an infinite number of selves, only some of whom attend Quantum.

"You remember that day, in the hall?" Aftershave says.

Weird. I do remember. One day, when I was student teaching, I was walking down the hall with three folders of essays on *Lord of the Flies*. I turned a corner and ran smack into Mr. Farquad. Calculus quizzes and book reports went flying. As we picked them up, Farquad told me he didn't envy my grading.

He had a point. Both my parents were high school teachers— my mother English, my father History. They used to come home with stacks of student essays. Sometimes they'd take sick days just to catch up on the grading. I used to swear I'd never turn into them.

But math? Math seemed so sterile. There was no magic in it. You couldn't cut the head off a Beanie Baby named Squealer, stick it on the end of a broomstick, and bring it into your class as a prop. Or pose important unanswerable questions, such as *Is Man Good or Evil?*, after Roger smashes Piggy's head in with a rock.

The rest of the table shares what they do. Mullet runs a dog kennel. Suit's a writer. Sarcasm a college adjunct. When Sarcasm talks about his job—contract exploitation, no benefits, food stamps—I consider changing his name to Bitter Me. He's the grad school version of myself. So glad I didn't get stuck there.

I could see myself in Suit, Aftershave, or Sarcasm, but Mullet? I remember joking once to Jane about quitting my job and doing something that required zero mental energy, like opening a dog kennel, but I wasn't serious.

Suit's the one I'm most interested in. The better version of me. I've written three screenplays, drawered in my desk at home. One about a sensitive white middle-class man stuck in a loveless marriage. One about a sensitive white middle-class man stuck in a dead-end career. And one about zombies.

"What do you write?" I ask.

"I'm a *ghost* writer," Suit says. "I just wrote Justin Bieber's memoir."

"Oh god."

Suit shrugs. "That shit sells."

"Yeah, but are you fulfilled?"

Everyone at the table looks at me. A beat. It's awkward.

Then they all crack up. Aftershave laughs so hard he spills his beer. Mullet slaps me on the back. I don't see what's so funny.

The reason I came to Quantum is simple: I want to find Perfect Me. Jane is skeptical about Perfect Me. She thinks he's like Bigfoot, a myth. I mostly agree with her. Except, when you think about it, there are an infinite number of unis in the multiverse, which means an infinite number of me. And somewhere in that infinity there's a me who made a right choice and then another . . . and another . . .

Only fifteen minutes at Quantum and I'm beginning to suspect Perfect Me might be more difficult to find than I thought. I'd settle for Happy Me. So, yeah, *fulfilled*.

"How much they paying you?" Sarcasm says.

"What?"

"The Multiverse Census."

Mullet snorts beer through his nose. It's like lunch duty in here.

"I don't get you guys," I say. "Isn't this what Quantum's all about? To get to know your alt selves and become better people?"

"Someone drank the Kool-Aid," Sarcasm says.

"That's how they *sell* it," Aftershave says.

"You think if any of us were *fulfilled* we'd be at Quantum?" Suit says.

"What do you mean?"

"Look around, Sad Eyes. You see any well-adjusted selves at this table? Colin here is a serial cheater; he's divorced four times. Then you got Colin, who won't have his student loans paid off until he's eighty. And behind door number three, there's Colin, who literally picks up shit for a living."

Jesus. This was not what I had in mind when I clicked that pop-up ad. This sad room full of me, nursing their drinks, trading miseries.

"Are *any* of you happy?" I ask.

Suit snorts. Sarcasm rolls his eyes. Aftershave chugs the rest of his beer.

Surprisingly, Mullet nods. "Mostly. Then again, it's like Colin said. I spend most of my day picking up shit."

"Then why do any of you come here?"

Suit shrugs. "To drink."

"To keep our selves company," says Sarcasm—the wit.

"To swap stories, measure dicks," says Aftershave.

"Plus," Mullet leans in, "there's a raffle later on."

◇◇◇

God. Is that what my laugh sounds like? I can't help wondering as their guffaws chase me out to the hall. I'm trying to find my way to the lobby, then back to my home uni, but somehow I get turned around. All the conference rooms look the same and I come around one corner too fast and slam right into a woman hurrying in the opposite direction. When I go to help her up I see that it's my wife.

"Jane! What are you doing here?"

And it topples down on me: she must have known I lied and followed me.

"Oh, honey," I say. "I'm sorry. I know you said this wasn't a good idea—and you were right—but I was stubborn and stupid and I had to see for myself. Can we please just go home and pretend this never happened?"

Jane frowns and looks at me funny. Her hair is different. Jane is always changing her hair. When she's stressed, she pops to her hairdresser and comes back with a different dye—Hot Toffee, Copper Shimmer, Sunflower Blonde. When she does something drastic, like a bob or a perm, I give her space. Now her hair is pulled back in a ponytail, only shorter—less pony, more rabbit. It's darker, too. A deeper shade of brunette than I'm used to, near black, with a tinge of purple. Blowout Burgundy?

"Did you go to the salon?" I ask. "How much—" but I stop myself. Our last few arguments have all been about money. Jane says she's beginning to feel like she lives in a Gestapo state run by our checkbook. And I don't really have a leg to stand on with my most recent purchase. When I showed her the QC website she said it was too expensive. I'd already bought a ticket.

Jane shakes her head and makes a *tsk tsk* noise I've never heard before.

"I'm sorry," she says. "Do I know you?"

I don't know whether to laugh or not. I settle for a dry chuckle. "Well, I'm only your husband."

"I've never seen you before in my life. What did you say your name was?"

"What is this—role play? Is that what we're doing?"

Jane and I tried role play once. We played Sexy Maid Fucked By Hot Plumber. It was a disaster. She kept breaking the fourth wall to get the story straight.

"So the Grishams are out strolling in the countryside when you come to fix the sink."

"The Grishams?"

"Yeah, they're the family that owns Billings Manor."

"Have you been bingeing *Downton* again?"

"No self-respecting woman would wear this in Present Day, Colin. Wait. Did they have plumbers back then? Maybe you could be an underbutler. Do you have any long underwear?"

"I thought you could just be dusting and I'd, you know, take you from behind."

"*Dusting?*" Jane laughed. "Rosalie's a lady's maid, Colin. Not a kitchen wench."

When Jane sets her mind on something, she goes all-in, which is why I'm not surprised she'd pretend to not know me to punish me for lying to her and attending Quantum. I don't realize I've taken her arm until she snatches it away.

"Jane?" I reach for her and she says, "Touch me again and I'll scream." She turns and rushes back down the hotel hall. I follow and she breaks into a full sprint. I feel like Jimmy Stewart in *It's a Wonderful Life.* The scene when George Bailey chases after his wife, Mary, a spinster librarian in the alt uni in which he was never born.

"Jane! It's me—Colin! Come on. We've been married for ten years!"

She slips into a conference room. I go in after her and suddenly I've stumbled into not one alt uni, but a roomful of them. A hundred Janes look up from their punch glasses, pause on the dance floor, break conversation to gape at me.

"Get away from me!" Rabbit Tail Jane shouts. She falls back dramatically in a faint. Two other Janes catch her.

I survey the room. A kaleidoscope of my wife's face on woman after woman.

"You need to leave," says Bodybuilder Jane.

"This is a *safe* space," says Cowgirl Jane. "No men."

"I'm sorry. It's just . . . is my wife here?"

Several other Janes come forward.

"Colin, darling," says Stepford Jane, touching her pearls. "What are you doing here? You're embarrassing me in front of my friends."

"Who's watching the kids?" says Mom Jane in her Mom Jeans and her Mom Cardigan, which is disturbing because we don't have any children.

"What the heck, Colin?" My Jane—or one who looks suspiciously like her—comes barrelling through the crowd. "I'm sorry," she says to the other Janes, looping her arm through mine. "I'll deal with him."

◇◇◇

Out in the hall, she drops my arm and digs around in her purse.

"Thank God," she says. "It's snoozeville in there."

"Jane?" I examine her. The hair's close enough. Same fashion sense, same smile.

"Yeah?" she says.

"No, I mean, are you My Jane?"

"You tell me." She surfaces from her purse with a pack of Nicorette gum.

"My Jane doesn't smoke."

She holds up the gum. "Neither do I."

I ask her if she knows the way back to the lobby and she leads me down the hall to an elevator. "Coming?" She holds the door for me.

"I, uh, think it's on this floor."

She smacks her gum furiously. I step in.

It opens on a hotel bar and restaurant.

Alt Jane sallies out. "The least you can do is buy me a drink."

◇◇◇

"I know," she sips her cocktail, "ask me something only she'd know the answer to."

"I don't think that works here," I say.

"Why not?"

"Well," I set down my beer. "When you think about it, there could be a Jane here who's exactly like my wife, only . . . I don't know, she didn't brush her teeth this morning."

"If that's all that separates me from your wife, we're practically the same person."

"Practically, not actually."

Alt Jane laughs and it's like time slips. "She has better oral hygiene."

"You laugh like her. My wife. Or how she used to."

"How does she laugh now?"

"I don't know. Less . . . full? She used to throw her head back like you do."

"Wow. You are *just* like My Colin."

"How so?"

She shrugs. "Devil's in the details."

So we sit and drink. I'm about ready to take the elevator down, find the lobby, and go home to My Jane, when Alt Jane says, "I know! Let's play a game."

"I'm not in the mood for games."

"Oh, come on. It'll be fun. It's called Never Ever. I'll be Your Jane and you'll be My Colin. We have to tell each other something we'd never ever tell our spouses."

"I don't know."

"I'll go first." She twirls the miniature umbrella in her drink. "Hmm . . . Okay. Colin, my sweet Colin. Never ever have I told you that I wish I'd married a man with a real job. You know, a *career*. A doctor or lawyer. A businessman—a guy in a suit! Not a wannabe artist, who basically babysits other people's kids and makes no money."

"Hey."

She chortles and claps. "Boy, that felt good. I've been holding onto that for a while. Okay. Your turn."

"I don't like this game." I move to get out of the booth.

"Oh, come on. I did it."

"I'm sorry. I don't know what to say."

"Look at me," she says. So I do. Her cheeks are flushed pink from the alcohol. She has on a bright turquoise necklace like the one My Jane wears. "Don't I look like her?"

"Well, yeah."

"Okay, then tell me. You have carte blanche here. Say what you've always wanted to say to her. I won't get mad."

I try to think of something harmless, a throw-away. "Sometimes I look at other women."

"That's it? Everyone does it. I bet you'd even tell her that. Come on, Colin. Don't you have something you'd like to get off your chest?"

"I've never cheated on her, if that's what you're getting at."

"Oh, Colin. I'm disappointed. I thought you'd have something better than that."

"Okay. How's this? Hi Jane. Guess what? I used the money you were saving for our second round of IVF to pay for this."

"For what?"

"This stupid doppelgänger convention!"

Others in the restaurant glance our way. I sink down in the booth. Alt Jane leans forward over the candle on the table. Shadows dance across her face.

"Oh, that's good," she says. "That's really good. Won't she find out?"

"I told her it was for car repairs. Parked the car at the mall for a few days. Took an Uber to work."

"That's so messed up. That's some serious deceit. I wonder if I can top it."

She mulls it over, signaling for the waiter to bring us another round.

"Okay. I got it." She reaches forward and takes my hand. "Colin, love. Never ever have I told you that I fantasize about Coach Farley when we're in the sack."

"Ugh," I take my hand back. "Are you serious? Matt Farley? That Neanderthal?"

"Sure."

"I bet he has back hair." My Jane thinks back hair is about the grossest thing a man can have. She told me this in bed, trailing her hand down my spine, after I'd said I wished I had more chest hair.

"Sometimes it's a turn on," Alt Jane says.

"And no one says *in the sack* anymore."

"I say *in the sack*."

"My Jane would never say *in the sack*."

"Well, I'm not *Your* Jane."

Our drinks come. A welcome distraction.

I take a swig; after this one, I'm out of here. "Matt Farley." I still can't believe it. "What a tool."

"It's your turn," she reminds me.

I don't know if it's the eight dollar beer or the idea of my sad schlockered selves getting more and more shitfaced together floors below us, or if I really want to shock her or if suddenly I've lost my grip and she *is* My Jane, but I finally come right out with it.

"All right. Here it is, Jane. How's it go? Oh, right. Never ever have I told you I don't want kids. Not through all the sperm tests and needle sticks. Not once did I bring it up. How after every pregnancy test, I prayed it would come back negative. How when you cried and I held you, all I felt was relief. Thank God, I thought. Another day for my life to be my own. But what life is that? Every day I drive to school I think of getting on the expressway and driving west and west and west until there's no more west. There's just water. I'd move to California. Work on my screenplays. Peddle them on the street. Bartend or wait tables to make rent. You think I don't know I'd be miserable? That a week in that life and I'd miss you terribly? Then why can't I stop think-ing about it? While you're sobbing over a pair of Baby Reeboks in Shoe Carnival, I'm blocking the goddamn scene in my head for a black comedy on suburban discontent! Every day I resent you for wanting more than me, even while I'm wanting more than you, too. How sick is that! You're the only goddamn thing I did right in my life. You. So if I can't figure out how to be happy with you, and I can't on my own, how the fuck am I supposed to do it with a child?"

Alt Jane's eyes widen. I know I'm making a spectacle of myself, but I can't stop. The other conference-goers shift their attention toward us and when I stand to leave I see that they're all Janes and Colins, each couple at a table with a little candle, a cocktail, and a beer.

Maybe they're married, attending Quantum together. But I doubt it. I bet each are from different unis, mixed and matched, all of them having conversations like Alt Jane's and mine—comparing relationships, taking notes.

You're not a special little snowflake. There are billions of snowflakes out there that are just like you. You couldn't be more insignificant.

Maybe later they'll end up in hotel rooms together. Maybe they'll recognize their spouses in the familiar way they are touched. Or maybe there will be just enough variation for it to be new, like when you and your wife come back to each other after so long apart, and you think, who are you? Where have you been all my life? Here, she tells you. Right here, all your life beside you. And you sigh in her arms. Oh, how I've missed you.

◇◇◇

I take the elevator down and wander the halls until I find the lobby. When I check out, the concierge gives me a complimentary swag bag with the QC logo.

I tell him I don't want it.

"But it's free!" He slides my black key card across the counter.

I take the card and leave the bag. I swipe the key in the Exit door and step through from the Marriott lobby to the Days Inn lobby in my home uni. I head out through the sliding doors to the parking lot. Before I can get to my car, my phone alerts me with a chain of texts and voicemails, all from Jane.

I rush home, knowing, but not knowing, and when I walk in she's in the kitchen and the way she rests her palm flat on her stomach, I know; I know and when she asks me where the hell I've been, before she can even give me the news, I tell her how happy I am.

The Keener

Three years ago, the day of our keening audition at St. Jerome's, the sisters lined us all up against the front wall of the orphanage after morning prayers. Mr. O'Grady, stinking of mutton and rattling change in his pockets, stood back while Ma Keener inspected our mouths, pressing down on our tongues one by one with a flat wooden stick that she wiped on her apron between girls. Then she told us to lament. We looked at each other.

"What's that?" Martha said.

"You know," Ma Keener said. "Cry for us."

"What for?"

"So we can hear your pretty voices. We can only take the two prettiest voices."

"But can't you hear them talking?"

"Martha," Sister Superior said and her eye itched on the tongue sticks like it sometimes did with rulers in class. Martha glanced away, but she didn't look down and she didn't say sorry. She was probably the bravest of all of us, but even she wouldn't cross the Supe.

"Now, I want you to think of something sad," Ma Keener said. "Something really really sad. Can you girls do that for me?"

Oh, could we. Dead fathers. Dead mothers. Dead sisters. Dead brothers. We close our eyes and what do we see? Bodies. Coffins. Holes in the ground. Lines of black hearses.

Sarah Beth was first in line. She's a screamer. The week before Ma Keener and Mr. O'Grady showed, she broke a dish cleaning in the kitchen and boy did she let loose. Something, anything, startles her like that and she gets this wide-eyed, terrified look on her face. There's a moment of blankness, of absolute surprise, and then her mouth drops like the little metal door on a mailbox and the heavens open like the Judgment's finally come.

"Go on, Dear," Ma Keener said. "Let's hear it."

If there had been a betting pool going, which was not unheard of at St. Jerome's, Sarah Beth would have had the best odds of anyone: Grade-A Keener Material. At some time or another she'd given all of us the shivers. Sisters leapt back in alarm, clutching to their chests a rolling pin, a laundry basket, a stack of Bibles, at finding Sarah Beth perched beneath their elbow, pale as a poltergeist, her hair a blonde curtain, parted for the round black stage of her scream.

Ma Keener raised her brow at Sarah Beth and we braced ourselves for a doozy. But the thing about keeners is that they have to cry on command. When we're standing at a grave, looking down at the coffin of a complete stranger, having to mourn their loss, there are no cold sheets to make us cry. No sad dripping showers. No broken plates.

Poor Sarah Beth never could hold up under pressure. Our gazes pinned her against the wall and the sad little thing *whimpered*. She cowered like a puppy. When we heard that pathetic puff of air we didn't want to comfort the miserable animal that made that sound. Our instinct was to hit it.

A good keener does not evoke pity in the listener, but solace— as Mr. O'Grady likes to say.

"Thank you, Dear," Ma Keener said, and she moved kindly down the line.

Sarah Beth hid behind her bangs and air unclenched from our lungs like fingers from fists. The Supe was clearly disappointed; she urged Ma Keener to try again, but this only made Sarah Beth retreat further into herself.

The Supe had been trying to rid St. Jerome's of Sarah Beth's scream for a long time. The Supe made other girls cry and we saw that girl's weakness, we watched her break, we looked on her with scorn. She made Sarah Beth cry and it was the Supe we glared at, the Supe we all hated.

Specs (prospective parents, Sister Adele always corrected us) came round and the Supe always led them right to Sarah Beth, who grudgingly got to her feet and introduced herself. We watched these encounters with jealousy, the Specs inspecting Sarah Beth like a used car.

It wasn't that anything would come of it; we knew she wouldn't be adopted; she wasn't one of the pretty ones. It was the attention that got us. The way the Specs fussed over her. Took her hand. Touched her cheek. Some of the women cried—the watery eyes kind that doesn't really count. Still. We envied Sarah Beth those tears. Even after, predictably, the Specs selected another.

"How about her?" they said inevitably, always, choosing the new girl, the pretty one, the one we never bothered getting to know.

"They'll eat her," Martha told us, sure of herself.

And sometimes, watching the nervous girl climb into the car, the too-nice way the Specs buckled her safely into the seat, we almost believed her.

When it was Martha's turn with Ma Keener, I knew it was going to be good. Martha would do just about anything to get out of St. Jerome's. There had been several botched escapes. Blankets tied together. Fences climbed. Two broken bones. She liked to pretend she didn't care about the Specs, she made a habit of rolling her eyes around them, but I'd seen her pinch her cheeks a little pinker, lick her hand and pat her bangs flat before the Supe led them through the kitchen.

There was a close call once. A few months before the auditions Martha pointed out the pretty one to a Spec and he struck up a conversation.

"*She's* the one you want," Martha said. "Just take her and go."

"How do you know *you're* not the one I want?" he said, only half joking. "Or *her?*" and he looked to the quiet girl sitting next to Martha. He looked at me.

"We're too old," she said. "I'm almost eight. She's seven."

We were both eleven. Although age wasn't the problem— it was looks that counted. And Martha was top-notch ugly. She had a birthmark that discolored the map of her forehead, a magenta continent her bangs only half hid. Her nose was potato-shaped, and she had bad acne scars on her chin. It was unusual for a Spec to look at her as openly as this one did. It was a good sign.

"You want a doll," she said to the Spec. "Not a girl. Not us."

"A regular Pinocchio," he said, laughing, and then, at our blank looks, stopping.

"What's that?" Martha asked.

"What? Pinocchio?" he said. "Little wooden boy? The puppet? You know—the fairytale."

"No," Martha said and she shook her head, fat fake tears welling in her eyes. "We don't know any fairytales. We don't have any mommies or daddies to read to us."

"Oh," he said and he looked at his hands. "Right."

"Just Bible stories," Martha said. "Noah and the Ark. Jonah and the Whale."

"There's a whale in Pinocchio, too."

"Maybe that's where they got it from," Martha said.

"Could be."

"The Supe says fairytales are the devil. But I don't think so."

"And why not?"

"Because it's not real," she said.

"What?" he said, smirking a little. "Fairies?"

"No," Martha said. "The devil."

"Oh," he said. I don't think he liked the sound of that.

"Only devil's people," Martha said, picking a sore on her chin.

"That's a funny thing to say. And fairies? Are they people, too?"

"Don't be stupid," she said. I could tell she immediately wanted to take it back.

"What about you?" the Spec asked me.

"She don't talk," Martha said and I looked the other way.

"Why not?"

"Don't feel like it, I guess."

The Spec smiled at me. "It's okay," he said. "Sometimes I don't feel like talking either."

I was warmed by the attention he paid me. In spite of my silence, Martha had hopes for me. I was plain-looking, she told me. She could work that angle. With a little personality, plain-looking could be almost pretty, she said. That's where she came in.

"Maybe you could tell it to us," Martha said. "About the doll and the whale. Please?"

"Yes," he said. "I'd like that."

But he didn't. The lady Spec he came with picked the pretty one and they left.

That night Martha cut off all her hair with a pair of pinking shears. Even the bangs. The geography of her birthmark fully revealed, her head looked to all like a world globe. She tied the shears to the back of her nightgown and woke everyone up, tottering up and down the dormitories between beds chanting: Wind me up! Wind me up! Wind me up!

Martha had a voice on her. Not as piercing as Sarah Beth's, but what it lacked in pitch it made up for in volume. Woke all of St. Jerome's that night.

She was determined that that very same voice would win her a ticket out. What her sweet-talking couldn't do she swore the breadth of her lungs could.

At Ma Keener's cue, Martha inhaled deeply, filling her lungs with the intensity of a flame burst in a hot air balloon, her ribs pressing outward like knives; she latched onto the breathe for seconds that held all of us in suspense, one . . . two . . . three . . . and then she released the loudest wail I ever heard. Like an ambulance siren breaking the calm of black city night: it wasn't chilling, it wasn't haunting, it wasn't moving in the least—what it was, was *deafening*.

The sheer power behind the cry was itself impressive, but even more alarming was how long she held it. Nostrils flaring, neck trembling, veins bulging in her eyes, Martha screamed. She screamed until her birthmark bled purple. She screamed until her mouth dried out. She screamed until her heart beat in her throat.

"Enough!"—that was the Supe.

"Goodness gracious!"—Sister Adele.

"My, oh my," Ma Keener said, hands over her ears. "Thank you, Dear."

Martha knew she'd failed. What she didn't know, what she couldn't know, was that keening is never a matter of wind. The loudest cry makes not the best keen, Mr. O'Grady likes to remind us. It's the voice's song that prevails, not its sails, he says. Every time.

"I could try it again," Martha said. "I could do it different."

"That's quite all right, Dear."

"I have lots of ways," she said. "Loud. Soft. Whatever you want."

She opened her mouth and let out a series of squawks. Fingers plugged ears. Cringes all around. Then a flash of white and the Supe had hold of Martha's arm—*whack!*

The last cry was real.

A silence followed. Back in line with the Sisters, the Supe gestured for the audition to continue. Ma Keener proceeded to me. I waited for Martha to intervene on my behalf, but she stayed quiet, clutching her wrist. Ma Keener signaled and I shook my head no.

"What's wrong?" Ma Keener said.

"Erin's a little shy," Sister Adele explained.

"She's a mute," the Supe said impatiently. "Move on."

Ma Keener stepped down the line and I felt a sharp pain at my scalp. Like something bit me. Barely enough time, a glimpse—fistfuls of my hair in Martha's hands—before they were diving back into the brown tangles, beasts in the underbrush. The madness with which her hands yanked my hair—it hurt it hurt it hurt! The contorted malice in the pursed concentration of her lips. She, my only friend, wrenching my head around in her fist, forcing me to my knees, so that I bowed to my audience, and in facing them, took in their looks, stunned by the beauty of my scream.

◇◇◇

Martha might have crossed her eyes and watched her own nose grow when she told the Spec we didn't know Pinocchio. It was not just our ages she'd lied about. Yes, there were Bible stories, but at St. Jerome's other yarns were spun, too.

See us now, the night before the auditions: heads on our pillows, minutes passing night, the sounds of lamps clicking off, steps receding down the hall, black habits retreating like shadows, a long uninterrupted silence, counting, counting, counting, and then—a floorboard creaks. The door opens and a figure, all in white, enters the room.

Twenty girls sit up in bed, gathering sheets around them like the trains of future wedding dresses. The book cracks, pages crease, a bookmark falls to the floor.

Sister Adele, her long dark braid hanging over a shoulder, had been reading to us in the stealth of night since she first came to St. Jerome's. She was the youngest of the Sisters; only five or six years separated her from our eldest. The night before the audition she'd chosen our entertainment carefully.

Sister Adele's story of the Banshee went like this:

Once there was a undertaker who had the most beautiful daughter. Every man in the village was struck by the girl's beauty and would have married her had it not been for a horrific deformity that revealed itself when they approached her in the town square and asked her name. For the girl had no tongue and could not speak, and when she opened her mouth to answer, the men saw that her gums were black and rotted and her appearance no longer pleased them. And so they withdrew their affections and the undertaker feared he might never find his daughter a husband.

On the daughter's thirteenth birthday, her mother was on her deathbed. She called the girl to her bedside to give her one last gift: the lullaby she once used to sing her to sleep, that had been passed down through the matrilineal line of their family, generation to generation, mother to daughter, for centuries.

The first time the lullaby was sung the night of her mother's death, the undertaker's daughter moved her lips silently to the words and her mouth was healed by the music. In the last note of the song the most beautiful voice ever heard in the kingdom rang out into the night.

The girl's mother made her daughter promise to sing at her grave every year, on the anniversary of her death, so that she might remember her poor mother's spirit and the love they once shared in life. But, her mother warned her, she must never sing the lullaby to any other or the consequences of her actions would be grave.

The second time the lullaby was sung that night it became a duet, sung by mother and daughter, together for the first and last time. As the ending note of the song faded on the mother's tongue, so too went her final breath.

And so the third time the song was sung that night the lullaby became a lament, a solo sung by the undertaker's daughter, whose grief spooled out of the house and into the night, down the road, past the cemetery, up the hill, and through the village square, where men everywhere stopped and listened: Husbands abandoned the embraces of their wives, shopkeepers closing up shop paused, keys in the latch, drunkards at the local tavern put down their pints of ale, and in the highest room in the highest turret of the castle, the widower king was awakened and rose from his goose-feather bed. Rubbing sleep from his eyes, he went over to the window, where he basked in the melody of the young woman's suffering in the light of a full moon. The king swore in that moment to find the woman who possessed the voice that had bewitched him and to make her his queen.

Elsewhere, a gravedigger rested from his task. Leaning heavily on his shovel, he wiped his brow. For him alone the spell of silence went unbroken.

When the undertaker heard the mourning song he went into the bedroom where he found his daughter washing his wife's body with her tears. He knelt before the girl. He took her hands in his. The song ended and he begged: again, again! But when she next opened her mouth he saw that it bled anew, as if the muscle that resided therein had been lopped off fresh. Over the course of a year the wound would slowly scab, and sweet decay would return to his daughter's breath until the organ was renewed, pinkly, on each anniversary of her mother's death.

What neither the undertaker, nor his daughter, understood was that this miraculous healing was not the only act of magic that night. For without knowing who or what she was, every man in the kingdom—save one—had fallen magically in love with the undertaker's daughter upon hearing her song. Neither she, nor her father, had an inkling of the spell she had cast. Worse, she did not know that it was the one un-enchanted of the lot, the gravedigger piling earth next to her mother's freshly dug grave, for whom her heart was destined.

Sister Adele closed the book there. Groans all around. She made a habit of cutting the story off when it was just getting good, to keep us all in anticipation for the next night. She made her rounds, tucking the youngest of us in, kissing each on the forehead.

"Tomorrow," she said. "You have to cry beautiful. Just like the undertaker's daughter. Can you do that for me, girls? Can you bewitch their hearts with your tears?"

Of course, we promised her. Anything for Sister Adele.

After she had gone I lay still a long time, thinking. I felt Martha, propped on her elbow in the dark, staring at me across the gap between our beds. There were nights I awoke to find her in bed with me, her black hair fanned across the pillow, the mark on her forehead pressed against my shoulder. I never knew when she came over; she always waited until everyone, including me, had fallen asleep. And in the morning she would be back in her own bed.

"You got to do it," she whispered. "I know you can."

I just lay there, eyes closed, counting breaths.

"I hear you in your sleep," she said. "Crying."

Was that why she came to me in the night? All this time I thought she was the one. That there was strength in my silence. If there were dreams, if there were nightmares, I did not remember them in the morning. She never touched me during the day. Who comforted whom?

"It's the saddest sound in the world," she said.

She wanted to go. She wanted so desperately to leave. And I all wanted was to stay here, safe, with her. How could I tell her? What would she say? The moon cast its yellow light on the floor slats. I sat up, slid over to the edge of the bed, and reached across. But she was already asleep.

"Martha," I said.

◇◇◇

There were three other seasoned keeners we joined, me and Sarah Beth. She'd made a surprise comeback: After it became clear to her that her whimper was not going to cut it with Ma Keener and Mr. O'Grady, she became distraught, and did what she did best (for once the Supe didn't mind).

So we make five. Mr. O'Grady handles the money, Ma Keener the girls.

A good keener is part talent and part training. Ma Keener used to be the best keener there was. That's how she got her name. Nobody knows what it was before. Katherine? Carolyn? All any of us know is that she used to keen so good that the name blended with the talent. That's how it is for us too. Mr. O'Grady doesn't bother with names. We're either "the girls" or "the keeners" to him, nothing more, nothing less.

When we look closely we can see how Ma Keener might have been pretty once. She has nice full lips and a long throat that could have been elegant if it weren't for all the wrinkles and age spots. Her hair's white-white, but in some light it looks white-blonde like it might have been when she was young. She's got to be at least fifty now and she can look a hundred.

She never sings anymore. Not even when we ask, practically beg. She's not like Sister Adele. There's hate mixed in with the love (if you can call it love). She trains us ("histrionic tutelage" she calls it) and when we do it right, when we nail the wail (as we call it), we can see in the way she purses those big lips that she's both proud and resentful. She misses her voice. She may still talk sweet—all them "Dears" and "Darlings"!—but the lilt's gone for good. All she got left is the croak.

I look at her and I wonder what will happen to us. If she used to be the best of the best, where will that put us once we're all grown up?

Mr. O'Grady is a fat greedy man, a villain right out of one of Sister Adele's fairytales. I never really believed Martha about the Specs eating the girls they adopted, but if anyone looks like an orphan-eater, it's Mr. O'Grady.

A skinflint too: he houses us in a one-bedroom apartment where we sleep on a single mattress, heaped in a pile, real cozy-like. Ma Keener has her own place, a closet of a room down the hall, so she can keep an eye on us. She brings us our meal, corn mash, maybe a little dumpling, every night. We share the bowl. Our stomachs grumble. Mr. O'Grady says it's good for business, it adds to the keen. Hunger and grief are only a few steps apart, he says.

It's not a hard job, the keening. The only one of us who ever had any real trouble was Sarah Beth, who still hadn't learned to cry on cue. During vocal training Ma Keener about gave up. She wanted to take her back to St. Jerome's.

"Can't we trade her in for another?" she asked Mr. O'Grady. "The poor Darling can wail like the dickens when she got something to wail about, but when she don't . . ."

"Don't worry," he said. "Give it time. She'll catch on."

Strange thing was, as much as Ma Keener complained about Sarah Beth to Mr. O'Grady, she never once brought me up. At those first training sessions Sarah Beth's screams fell flat, but I didn't cry at all. It was the only protest I had, my silence. I wanted to go back to St. Jerome's. To Martha. To Sister Adele. And I thought the only way to do that was to keep my mouth good and shut.

"Now don't be obstinate, Dear," she said. "We've all heard your lovely voice."

I drew my lips to a line, locked them with my finger, threw away the invisible key.

Ma Keener's frustration was a crackling noise—dry twigs snapping across knees.

She tried Martha's trick. But I was ready for it this time. Ma Kenner yanked hard, much harder than Martha had, hair ripped out in great clumps, but I only bit my lip. Harder she pull, harder I bit, till I tasted blood, but not defeat.

"Fine," she said, huffing a little. "Don't you worry your pretty head, Dear. If I have to pull every last strand, I'll find a way."

And she did. Ma Keener was a problem solver. With our first show coming up (it was always "the show" to Ma Keener; she refused to use the f-word) she was desperate as ever. She'd grown so tired of Sarah Beth's feigned cries, she lashed out one rehearsal—struck the girl across the face. Startled, Sarah Beth began to cry, real tears this time, and instantly the room grew colder. Pleased, Ma Keener went in for another, hand raised like a fly swatter, so I knocked her down.

She's mean, but she's not strong. She dropped like a bag of bones, and to everyone's surprise she laughed a wheezy gasp of a laugh. She sent the other girls out of the room, but she kept Sarah Beth and me behind.

Cry for me, she said and I just turned my head. So she went to Sarah Beth and carefully plucked one lock of her golden hair. Sarah Beth screamed. I stepped forward, not thinking, and it came out—"don't!"

"It speaks," Ma Keener smiled. "Thank you, Dear."

She pulled again: the scream, the scream, that awful scream! Sarah Beth thrashed in her arms, and I knew there was only one way to stop it, only one thing I could do without hurting someone, and so I unlocked my lips, I unhinged my jaw, and I cried. Sarah Beth's and my screams blended, harmonious, and only after the echo of that one pure sound resonated through the walls of the run-down apartment building did Ma Keener let go.

She was not always so cruel. The morning of the first show Ma Keener brought over a cardboard box to the apartment. Inside we found black clothing: dresses, skirts, sweaters, cloaks, coats, shawls. Ma Keener helped us pick through these, like we were backstage at a fashion show. The three more experienced keeners, whose own funereal garb was already stashed in the corner of the room, stood us in front of the cracked bathroom mirror.

It became a morbid game of dress-up. Sarah Beth spun around the room like a top. She sashayed her hips as if her ragged pinafore were a cocktail gown. She untangled a knot of black veils, draping them over her face like mosquito netting. The other keeners, even Ma Keener, played along. Every so often we laughed. We could be bridesmaids going to a wedding.

One of the elder keeners tossed me a dress.

"Should fit you," she said. "You're about Marie's size."

The dress pooled at my feet and I stepped into it like a puddle of dark water. I did not ask who Marie was or what had happened to her.

When we had finished dressing Ma Keener led us out of the apartment, down the stairs, out to the street. The cemetery was not far. We walked. We met Mr. O'Grady at the corner and followed him and Ma Keener in a straight line.

We looked to all the world like a set of black chess pieces. Pawns.

◇◇◇

It's been three years now. Today's show is for some rich Comte. Mr. O'Grady's expecting a big payday. He even came to our rehearsal (we don't rehearse anymore; we know what we're doing) so Ma Keener had to put on a little show of her own.

"I want a melancholic spectacle," he says during his pep talk. "A real outpouring of emotion. Make them weep."

Wailing. That's what we call it. Like on a guitar. Screech it, we say, before we go on. Like it's all in good fun. Screech it. Oh yeah.

When we arrive at the cemetery, the gravesite's almost empty. A dead man's obviously not well liked when five of the eight at his funeral are strangers paid to cry for him. Besides the priest there's only one mourner: a young man in a stiff black suit.

The Comte's son? I wonder. He doesn't look particularly sad.

What a day for a funeral. I hope mine's half as nice. Freshly mown grass. Clear sky. Warm breeze. Most people hear funeral and think rain. Umbrellas. Dead leaves. They wax romantic about the weather like it should set the mood. Well, I've been to my fair share of burials and trust me: the sun mourns for no one.

I'm comfortable around graves now. When you spend all your time in a cramped apartment with four other girls, cemeteries feel like parks. Here I can breathe.

The show starts with a little blubbering. The priest reads from his black leather Bible and we perch around the coffin like stuffed crows. Sarah Beth whimpers at the mention of heaven. The keeners sigh when the priest offers his blessing. Then, almost silently at first, the tears come.

I can't stop staring at the man in the black suit. He looks neither at the priest, nor the coffin, but out across the graveyard, his hands in his pockets, his shoulders hunched.

One of the more dramatic keener girls lets out a wail too soon.

A good keener knows timing. She builds her grief like a wave. She rides the swells before crashing down. She doesn't lose herself to hysterics.

The priest talks of the Comte like an old friend. A good business man, he says. Put everything into his work. Respectable.

The girls begin to sob now. Their crying enters a new register, reaching a fever pitch. Sarah Beth's pierces. Screech it, sister.

The coffin is lowered. A girl beside me, caught in the moment, falls to her knees. She beats the ground. She tears up fistfuls of grass. Strings of saliva dangle from her chin.

The Comte's son takes a handful of dirt and throws it in.

Here I scream. It's how the show ends. Ma Keener saves me for last.

What do I think of when I keen? Where does the cry I heave, like a bucket from a well, come from? You're probably thinking Martha or Sarah Beth or Sister Adele or maybe the ghost of my parents, a family I've never known, faces conjured by my mind. And, yes, perhaps it was once so.

But I no longer think when I keen. I feel a permanent stone lodged in my throat and I know the reflex is there, safe, ready whenever I need to call on it. Even Sarah Beth, who we once pinched discreetly beneath her black coat, little red marks on the back of her arms, even she has found a way to make do.

For all of us it has become second nature. We sing together and it's like playing a recording of ourselves. I look into all the gaping mouths that surround me and I lose my own voice somewhere in the collective scream.

But when I take in a breath the dead man's son looks at me and the stone in my throat catches. I see how he hates me. He hates all of us. He knows what a sham we are.

Without my voice to support them my sister keeners falter. Mr. O'Grady senses something amiss, an absent note in the chord. The priest closes his Bible and the show flatlines.

Ma Keener takes hold of my hair. She hasn't dared touch me in years. I brace for pain, but it doesn't come. She lets go. The Comte's son is walking toward us.

"That was something," he says to Mr. O'Grady.

"Thank you, sir," Mr. O'Grady says.

The Comte's son talks business for a minute, the issue of a will, bank accounts, checks. Then, strangely, he turns to me and asks if I might care to go for a stroll.

Ma Keener is speechless. Mr. O'Grady stammers.

"A short one," the Comte's son says. "Just around the grounds. I'll bring her back safely," he promises and then he holds out his arm: a proper gentleman.

I take it, heart pounding.

We stroll (Stroll! When have I ever strolled? The idea of it!) along the path and an awkward tension settles between us. In the silence that descends a strange idea occurs to me. I look closely at the headstones so as not to watch him watching me and an elaborate fantasy unwinds quickly inside me so that before I can stop myself it's leapt from my mouth:

"Are you going to adopt me?"

He laughs. "Heavens no," he says. "Where did you get such a notion? Sounds like something straight out of Dickens."

"What's that?"

"What? Dickens? You've never heard of Dickens! He's a novelist. He writes about, well, his books are about orphans."

"Oh. Is that why you wanted to talk to me?"

"In a way. I find you curious," he says. "I'm a writer, too. It's a bit of a hobby. I was hoping you might tell me what it's like. Maybe I could get a story out of it."

"I don't know what it's like," I say, thinking of the gravedigger from Sister Adele's fairytale. "I never knew my family."

"No, no, no," he says. "Not orphans. *Keeners.* What's it like to cry at a funeral for someone you've never even met?"

"It's not hard," I say.

"But you didn't cry like the others," he says. "Why not?"

"I don't know," I say. "I just. Couldn't."

"Do you often? Find you can't?"

"Do you?"

He doesn't answer. The question seems to confuse him. I take my arm back.

"Let me ask *you* something," I say. "Why don't you cry at your own funerals?"

"Oh, I don't know. It's unseemly. It doesn't look good."

"I don't know," I say. "I think you could cry pretty if you wanted. For your father."

"My *father?* That's not my father."

"Then who is he?"

"The Comte? My uncle. He was not a very popular man."

"You didn't love him?"

"He was a real bastard. He screwed a lot of people over. All he cared for was money. There won't be a need for keeners at my father's funeral. He has friends."

"That's good," I say.

"I won't need them at mine either," he says. "I'm going to get married and have a big family and my wife and kids will miss me so much, they'll cry so hard they'll wake the dead."

"That's good too."

"You're kind of pretty, you know."

I look at my feet.

"I'm glad you didn't cry," he says. "You looked sadder than the whole lot of them and you didn't shed a tear. That's very impressive. You made me feel almost sad for him."

"Everyone should make someone sad when they die," I tell him.

"Do you know the story of the banshee?" he asks.

Martha, I think. Pinocchio. Sister Adele. I shake my head no.

"Well," he says. "Legend has it there's an old hag who lives in the woods. And she's blind except for she can see how a person's going to die. And when she sees that death happen, she goes out of the woods and into the villages where she stands outside the family's cottage and cries to let them know death is coming. She's the first to mourn for the loss. Some people say that her song is what kills, but I don't believe it. I think she's good. I think she's just warning them."

I think of how sometimes, when nightmares wake me, I untangle myself from my sisters in their yawning sleep. I get up from the mattress we share and I go to the bathroom down the hall. I sit on the tiles, but I don't turn on the light. I am watching the dark. I am listening to the night. I feel it inside me, her banshee wail, but I won't let it out.

"Her song is beautiful," I say.

"Like you," he says and he raises his index finger, touches the corner of my eye, tracing a line down my cheek.

"Banshee," he says.

◇◇◇

Before we left the orphanage, Sister Adele, Martha, and the other girls came to our dormitory, where Sarah Beth and I were packing, to say goodbye. Sarah Beth pulled and pulled on the hem of Sister Adele's habit, begging her to tell the end of the banshee story before we left St. Jerome's for good.

"What happened to the undertaker's daughter?" she pleaded.

Sister Adele did not have time to retrieve the book and so she told us quickly, from memory.

"Why, she marries the prince, of course," she said. "She goes back to her mother's grave and she sings the song again and he finds her and she lives happily ever after. Just like you girls."

"You mean the window king?" Sarah Beth said.

"Widower," Martha corrects her. "But what about the gravedigger?"

"Oh, yes, well," said Sister Adele. "It would never have worked between them. He was immune to her spell."

"Why?"

"He was deaf."

"You mean," Sarah Beth said with a scared look. "Like the Grim Reaper?"

"No, no. Deaf. It means he couldn't hear."

"Why not?"

"He was born that way."

"But I thought they were destined for each other," Martha said and she took my hand.

"Yeah," Sarah Beth said. "Did she even love that window king?"

Sister Adele hesitated. "Of course she did," she said. "She loved him very much. And she sang beautifully for him just like you girls will too. Very soon."

What do you mean she sang? What about her tongue? What about the spell? What about her mother's warning? Was that really the end? We wanted to know. Please, we begged. Tell us the truth.

But Sister Adele just smiled.

◇◇◇

The undertaker's daughter kept her mother's promise and visited her grave on the anniversary of her death for three years. Every time she was healed only long enough to sing the lullaby to her mother's ghost three times.

And every year on the very same night the king searched the village for the owner of the voice he'd fallen in love with. He went door to door and asked every maiden in his kingdom to sing the words he now knew by heart. But each time he came to the undertaker's home the girl answered the door only to reveal her mouth, returned to its blackened state. And so her secret was kept.

On the third year the gravedigger was burying a coffin on the night of the ritual. He spied the undertaker's daughter, kneeling at her mother's grave, and he read her lips, but felt not the power of her song. When the lullaby ended and the girl stood, she discovered the gravedigger, but she could not speak to him. And he could not hear her.

She fell in love with him immediately, for only he could resist the magic of her song, only he could love her purely, his love for her untainted by her mother's spell.

And so she brought him back to her father for his blessing. But the undertaker refused to allow the marriage. A gravedigger was too poor for his daughter. The lovers didn't care; the grave-digger told him that with or without his blessing they planned to elope.

But the undertaker had made other plans that night; for while the daughter tarried in the cemetery with the gravedigger, he had been the one to answer the king's call. And he told the king he knew exactly who he searched for.

There was a knock at the door. It was the king's men, come for the girl. Before the lovers might escape, they were arrested and brought before the king. He bade the undertaker's daughter to sing, but she kept her mouth shut for love.

And so the king held a knife to her lover's throat and asked again. Knowing full well her mother's warning, the undertaker's daughter had no choice but to sing the lullaby so that her mouth was healed and the beautiful song echoed through the king's chamber and he knew he had found his queen. He did not wait for her song to end before he slit the gravedigger's throat.

The undertaker's daughter screamed. She screamed and the king knew her wrath. He was killed instantly by the shriek and he was not the only victim. Like her mother's song, the scream carried and the other occupants in the castle too heard her mourning cry, and the villagers it drifted down to felt its blade, and even the undertaker, her father, alone in his cottage, guilt-ridden at what he'd done, fell prey to its murderous rage.

The girl knelt before her slain lover and kissed his cold lips. She closed his eyes, then rose to her feet. She fled the kingdom and the massacre she'd caused, she walked down the stone stairs and out of the castle, she passed by the carnage her cry had left in its wake, the empty village, bodies lying facedown in the street. She followed the road, beyond the cemetery, past her father's cottage, and into the woods, never to be seen again.

Not Nobody, Not Nohow

Early morning, the first official day on set, Maggie witnessed her transformation in a long mirrored wall. The make-up artist's hands darted back and forth as he brushed glue onto the tips of her nose and chin, attached rubber pieces from molds, and applied liberal swatches of green paint to her face, neck, and hands. In Costuming, she was pinched by a clutch of fitting girls, a black pointed hat bobby-pinned to her long braided hair. Props handed over her broomstick, twigs frizzing out the end like a bad perm. They told her to head to the screen test in fifteen.

As she crossed the studio lot, she was stopped several times: first by two stagehands, who fell to their knees facetiously, begging her not to turn them into toads; then by Mr. LeRoy, the producer, who took her by the shoulders and held her at arm's length to admire the make-up—"Movie magic in the making!" he beamed; and finally by Miss Garland, who in one melodramatic movement, dropped the script she was holding, put her hands to her cheeks, and let out a shrill little scream that soon dissolved into a fit of giggles.

"Oh, Maggie!" she said. "You look absolutely evil!"

"I'll take that as a compliment," Maggie said. She struck a mock-villainous pose, holding out a clawed hand to show off her false fingernails. That earned her a laugh.

She had only recently met Miss Garland at a cast meeting, but already the girl seemed to be good fun. Judy was sixteen, twenty years her junior. Maggie had seen her in two films starring Mickey Rooney. She had a truly remarkable voice. And such stage presence. Maggie could scarcely hope to match her talent in front of the camera.

"It's positively ghastly, that's what it is!" Judy said. "Oh, but it suits you, Maggie. Really it does!" She made a habit of turning up the end of her sentences so everything came out exhilarated, bouncy. It would work well for her character, who was the very definition of innocence.

"I should hope not," Maggie suppressed an impulse to touch the false wart they'd stuck on her chin.

Judy stepped back. She shook her head, realizing her mistake. "Oh no. Not like that," she said, blushing. "I didn't mean it like that!"

"Of course not," Maggie smiled. She bent down and picked up Judy's script for her. "See you at the screen test." She hefted her skirt like a black parachute over her gray-stockinged legs, and continued on her way to her dressing room—which was really more of a tent.

The canvas flapped closed behind her and she put the broom down on the little card table in the corner. She rummaged through her purse until she found a compact. When she flipped it open she let out a little cry of her own—half delight, half fright. Even after sitting in a chair in Make-Up for two hours, she still wasn't used to it. Maggie brought the little mirror closer, having to remind herself that the green face staring back was, in fact, her.

Ghastly was right. She certainly looked the part, with her high forehead and long aquiline nose. It was her mother's word, *aquiline.* A word used to describe the noses of Roman emperors. "It's regal," she'd told her, but Maggie knew what it really was. *Hooked.* She had the nose of a witch, and the make-up artist had emphasized this. Her look suited the character so well, it was a wonder she hadn't always seen it, the evil in the contours of her face, and that she'd been confused by her casting when her agent first called about the part.

"Maggie," he'd said. "They want you for a part on *The Wizard.*"

"*The Wizard?*" she said. "*The Wizard—of Oz?*"

She'd heard that MGM was adapting L. Frank Baum, but she'd never imagined there was a part in it for her. Maggie was a character actor. She was used to bit parts: Mossy the Maid, Drugstore Lady #1. She was typically cast in the role of the spinster: mean old broads living in New England Victorians. She played Edna, Agatha, Hester. Crotchety, that's what her face read.

Her looks were plain and she would never attain the fame a talent like Judy was destined for, but the work was fun and the pay sure beat her teacher's salary.

"That's wonderful!" she said to her agent. "What's the part?"

"You'd be the lead. Well, one of them."

"Just tell me already."

"The Witch," he said.

"The Witch!"

He laughed. "What else, Maggie? Obviously, you can't play the little farmgirl."

She didn't know whether to be grateful or offended. The Witch?

"Wait a minute." She'd read something in the paper. "I thought Gale Sondergaard got that part."

"Not exactly. They were considering her, but now they say she's too pretty."

"Ha! Too pretty! That's a first."

"Listen, Maggie. This could be big for us."

"I mean, isn't that what make-up's for? They add a little blemish here, a little there, and *voila!* they turn beauty into the beast."

"Maggie, are you listening? Rumor is this is MGM's *Snow White*."

"And *Gale Sondergaard* turned it down?"

"Apparently. But I've heard it was the producers' call. Even with all the make-up, they say she's too attractive. She was expecting the part to be like Disney. You know, beautiful, like the evil queen. But they want a crone."

Maggie snorted. "Boy can you flatter a girl, or what! So. When do I start?"

◇◇◇

He finds the shoes at the bottom of his mother's closet, a gaudy pair of red pumps he stuffs with tissue. The tutu is his sister's. She's almost ten now; she gave up dance two years before, moving on to less feminine hobbies—soccer, softball, tennis. The dance costume is blue-sequined with white frill, but to him it's a plain frock of blue-and-white gingham. It fits about right.

It's the summer of his sixth birthday, a summer he spends watching *The Wizard of Oz* on repeat, holed up in the basement living space—pull-out couch, storage closet, a small bathroom with peeling brown wallpaper and a broken mirror. The tape has permanently lodged in the VCR, rewound so many times a few scenes—like the one with the apple-throwing trees—have grown staticky at the corners.

Day after day, the boy acts out the story with the movie. He likes climbing on the edge of the couch, balancing as Dorothy Gale does on the fence of a pig pen, then collapsing onto a pre-stacked pile of cushions. He tornadoes around the basement, knocking books and photographs from shelves. He dives under the couch so only his feet stick out, as if a house has fallen on him.

When Dorothy opens the door to reveal Oz after crash-landing in Munchkinland, he closes his eyes tight and reopens them, pretending he's seeing the world's color—orange shag carpet, forest green walls, yellow rocking chair—for the very first time.

At the end of the movie he clicks his heels three times and even though he knows this won't do anything, he always hesitates before that final click, and for a moment he believes the shoes might take him somewhere, somewhere wonderful—but where?

He's already home. He's always home. There's a babysitter that watches him and his sister: a teenage boy from down the street. The babysitter lifts the boy's father's weights in the garage every morning and works in the yard, mowing, mulching, planting, every afternoon. He makes the boy and his sister tuna fish sandwiches on toasted wheat bread for lunch. Wednesdays, he takes them to the neighborhood pool.

The boy's sister is in love with the babysitter. While the boy runs around the backyard crying Toto! Toto!, she spends the summer reading in the babysitter's proximity. In the morning, while he lifts, she reads *Little Women* on the front porch in full view of the open garage. In the afternoon, she reads *The Secret Garden* out back on the deck while he weeds. At lunch, she reads *Gone with the Wind* at the kitchen table, glancing over the book's cover at the babysitter, who scans the Sports page, pickle relish on his chin.

"What?" he says. "Something on my face?" He picks up a napkin and rubs, which only smears the relish more.

"No," the boy's sister says and she retreats behind her book.

The boy sits in his tutu; the red shoes hang over the edge of his seat, dangling below the kitchen table like ripe fruit. He swings his legs back and forth humming "Somewhere Over the Rainbow," crunching on potato chips. His parents and sister, and even the babysitter, have grown used to this.

The first time the babysitter came over the boy's parents showed him around the house; the boy's mother opened the basement door, revealing the boy skipping down below, around and around like a dog in a pen. The carpeting showed signs of wear, a track circling the perimeter of the room where the heels had torn the rug up: a carpet moat.

"He loves to play his imaginary games," she said. "If he gets out of line just say 'poppies.' He pretends to fall asleep. Should buy you a few minutes. 'Snow' wakes him up."

"He doesn't really like sports," the father said. "But if you could find something the two of you could do together. I don't know, like videogames or something . . . it would be nice."

So the first day the parents were gone the babysitter called the boy into the garage and put a five-pound weight in his hand. He ignored the tutu.

"What am I supposed to do with this?" the boy said.

"Lift," the babysitter said. He demonstrated an arm curl with a dumbbell, back hunched, head bent so close to his bicep it looked like he might kiss it. "Okay. Your turn."

The boy performed a tiny curl of his own, then set the weight back down.

"Can I go and play now?"

"Don't you want to be big and strong?" said the babysitter.

"I'm only six."

"So? How are you going to get any chicks with that attitude?"

This confused the boy. What did he want chickens for? He'd rather have a flying monkey.

"Can you do a push-up?" the babysitter asked and the boy shook his head.

"I can plié," he said. This was true; his sister had showed him once.

"What's that?" the babysitter said.

The boy assumed the position, pliéd.

"That some kind of aerobics?" the babysitter said.

The boy shrugged.

"Look, if you want to do a push-up, you're going to have to take off those shoes. The dress can stay, I guess, but the shoes have to go. So you can balance on your toes."

"No!" the boy shouted, a little more forcefully than he'd meant, and he ran into the house. The babysitter lay back down on the bench press. He didn't try again.

On Wednesday, the boy stands on the edge of the pool deck wearing a pair of scuba diving goggles, skin tinged ghostly white from sunscreen. Neighborhood kids hop barefoot all around. He gazes down at the water, looking like he's fashioned a set of flippers from two red delicious apples.

"Poppies," the babysitter says to him, and the boy does a little pirouette, flapping his mouth open like a little door and stretching his arms high above his head in a fake yawn. At the end of the turn he pinches his nose closed and falls face-first, belly-flopping into the water, where he floats on his stomach like a dead man. The babysitter will have to go wake him up with "snow" before he drowns. If he knows anything about the boy, he knows his commitment to his fantasies.

He carries the boy spluttering out of the pool, sets him down on the edge of the lounge chair and dumps out the water and damp tissue from the high heels. He says, "snow," and the boy blinks his eyes open, rising slowly. He brushes at his shoulders and hair, looking up to the sky, cupping his hand, the motion so real, the babysitter can almost envision him catching snowflakes.

"Unusual weather we're having, ain't we?" the boy says.

In the chair beside him, his sister rolls her eyes. "You are so weird."

◇◇◇

At the screen test Maggie practiced moving in her long skirt and cape. The costume designer rarely asked her opinion as he watched her saunter in front of the camera, commenting on the look of her dress's sleeves and collar.

"How's the make-up feel?" Mr. LeRoy asked.

Maggie had no idea how sensitive an issue this was until years later when she found out about the wardrobe debacle that had been the Tin Man costume. Poor Buddie Ebsen had an allergic reaction to aluminum dust he'd inhaled and had to be hospitalized. He was replaced by Jack Haley, lickety-split. Everyone assumed MGM had fired Ebsen, but didn't know why.

Maggie knew to be agreeable in big productions like this, so she told the producer she liked her coloring just fine. It was mostly true. Her make-up dried comfortably enough without cracking, but she couldn't touch anything—her dress, door handles, toilet seats—without fear of leaving a green smear behind.

Judy joined her soon after Maggie's initial shots with the flying monkey, which—no matter how often she told herself it was just a little man—gave her the heebie-jeebies.

"Hi, Maggie!" Judy said. She was wearing a ridiculous blonde wig and her face was heavily rouged. "Isn't this exciting?"

"Don't you look lovely," Maggie smiled.

"Oh, I don't know," Judy said. She twisted a long, golden curlicue around her finger. "Not as pretty as Shirley Temple, I'd say."

"Well, I wouldn't," Maggie said. Shirley Temple had been considered for Judy's part, but Twentieth-Century Fox had refused to loan her to MGM. "You're every bit as talented as her. And you can sing better too."

"You think?" Judy said, tilting her head.

The screen test went well. Maggie rushed around looking menacing and Judy cowered in mock fear. They enjoyed each other so much, it became difficult for Judy to act scared; she kept laughing when Maggie said something in the Witch's voice.

"You're too nice!" Judy kept telling her. "Stop being so nice!"

When there was a lull in the attention the director, producers, and designers were paying them, Judy asked Maggie if she was married. It was a question Maggie's own mother would have scolded her for asking a stranger, but she was secretly charmed by Judy's curiosity.

"I was," Maggie told her. "But it didn't work out. I don't mind though, because I got something better out of it. My son. Hamilton. You'd like him. He's a real sweetheart."

"Does he get birthday parties?" Judy asked.

"Of course. But he's only had two. On the last one we had a chocolate cake and—"

"When I was little I never had birthdays," Judy said. She twirled her little handbasket, the one where the pet dog would go. "I never had a best friend. And I never got to do any clubs."

"Oh. I'm sorry."

Judy shrugged. "One time I was on a train and I looked out the window and I saw three little girls playing with baby dolls, and I thought—looks like fun. And that's when I knew I missed out on my childhood."

"Goodness." Maggie was beginning to get the impression that, like so many stars, Judy demanded an audience both on and off stage.

"We were terribly poor," Judy monologued. "We went from town to town and I sang to make money. I never got to go to school. My dream is to graduate from Hollywood High next year. I've already got my dress picked out and everything."

"I'm sure the movie will be done by then."

Over the following weeks, Maggie overheard the costume girls making fun of her co-star. The girls struck poses in mirrors, pouted sarcastically, and talked in baby-girl voices.

"It's *so* not fair," one said. "I *never* got to play in the sandbox when I was a kid because I had to sing for the Emperor, His Majesty, until I went absolutely *hoarse*."

"Well, when I was little, we were so poor my mama made me *tap dance* to keep warm."

"If only I wasn't so beautiful and talented, then maybe someone would love me."

"Hey," Maggie said. "Give the poor girl a break. She's under a lot of pressure."

The costume girls shared glances.

"Please tell me you don't actually buy into her sad, misunderstood movie-star act."

"I had to refit her three times on her last picture. The stunts she pulled? Slouching and holding her breath so the waist would come back an inch too short and have to be taken out again."

"*Girls*," the costume designer said, and they went back to their pinning.

Maggie ignored them. She felt bad for Judy. She even asked to see her graduation dress.

It was a simple, white dress, and Judy modeled it in her dressing room. Maggie told her she could envision her on stage already, awarded her diploma, tossing her graduation cap high into the air. Judy performed a little slapstick routine in which she accepted an invisible scroll and curtsied, moving an imaginary tassel from one side of her cap's mortarboard to the other. Maggie laughed.

"You'll come, won't you?" Judy said. "Please say you'll come!"

"I'd love to," Maggie said, and Judy hugged her.

But it was months before May, and Maggie had forgotten all about her promise until after the film was complete. At breakfast one day, she picked up the newspaper and saw that MGM was

sending Judy on a personal-appearance tour on the date scheduled for her graduation. Maggie was so upset about it she called
a contact of hers in MGM's publicity department to ask if the
studio was letting Judy off to attend, but her friend said she didn't
know anything about it.

The next time she saw Judy in person was at the *Oz* premiere
at Grauman's Chinese Theatre in August, but her co-star had
been perpetually surrounded by reporters, fans, and flashbulbs,
too busy preparing for her live performance with Mickey Rooney
to speak with Maggie.

He's happy that entire summer. It's the last he'll ever know such
happiness. He starts school in the fall and his parents worry when
the Oz phase hasn't worn itself out by the end of August. His
dance costume shows the wear of that summer: the tutu hangs
limply from his hips like mosquito netting, the shoulder straps
dangle like deflated balloons, the blue sequins dulled from dust in
the basement, stained by grass from his play in the backyard. The
shoes, his ruby slippers, are scuffed, the heels broken off, super-
glued back on twice.

The night before school starts his parents come into his room
and sit next to him on the bed. The costume is laid out on a chair
with the red shoes under it.

"Have you picked out what you want to wear tomorrow?" his
mother says.

The boy motions, but she shakes her head. She gets up, goes
to the dresser, opens drawers.

"What did we say?" his father says. "You can't wear that to
school."

His mother comes back to the bed with several T-shirts and
shorts. She begins laying out the options. The boy buries his head
into his pillow.

"Hey now," his father says. "You can put it back on when you come home from school, okay? How does that sound?"

The boy doesn't know how that sounds. All he knows is that his parents are upset and he's scared because tomorrow is the big day, but he doesn't want to go. He wants to stay here with his sister and the babysitter, and he wants to watch his favorite movie and wear the ruby slippers, because they make him feel good and why do things have to change?

"How about this one?" his mother says, holding up a red shirt with a black swirl of stars.

"Don't you want to go to school where you can make friends?" his father says.

He doesn't. He really doesn't. When he thinks about the other kids all he can see is a crowd of Munchkins, dancing and singing about how dead the Witch is now that Dorothy's dropped a house on her. He hates that part, almost as much as he hates when the guard at the Emerald City tells Dorothy she can't see the Wizard—*Not nobody, not nohow!*—and she starts to cry, because they came all that way, and now she'll never get home.

But the absolute worst is when the Witch melts. The boy's scared of the Witch; he doesn't like her because she's mean to Dorothy, but he doesn't like the killing even more. There's something gruesome about the way the Witch turns into a steaming puddle, even if it is an accident. Dorothy's always causing accidents. He usually fast-forwards through that scene.

"You have to be brave tomorrow," his mother says. "Like the Cowardly Lion. Find your courage. Can you do that?"

He doesn't even like the Lion. The Scarecrow is his favorite. And his mother's already told him over and over about getting brains at school for his diploma. Like when the Wizard makes the Scarecrow super smart at the end.

He sinks deeper into the bed, rubs away their kisses on his cheeks and forehead, and turns toward the wall in the dark.

In the morning he will put on the red shirt. His mother will rub gel in his hair and do it in spikes like he used to like. She'll help him put on his backpack and he'll stand with his sister while his father takes their picture: his sister, holding up two bunny ears behind his head, and the boy, with his blue lunchbox, looking down at his sneakers.

◇◇◇

In Maggie's first scene she felt like a crow, pecking back and forth on the sound stage, from the house atop her supposedly dead sister, the Wicked Witch of the East, to the center of the Munchkin pavilion, where Billie, in that ridiculous bubblegum pink costume, stood protectively by Judy. The little people cowered in their silly flowerpot hats and curlicue wigs, lying flat on the swirl of yellow brick like the victims of a mass fainting spell, and Maggie pointed and cackled and threatened as the camera panned, a sweeping black vision.

Judy, in pigtails—they'd decided to do without the wig—and bright lipstick, stood smack dab on her mark, radiating childhood. "I thought you said she was dead," she said to Billie, who in her Titanic of a dress looked less like a fairy godmother than a mountain of cotton candy. Billie was in her fifties and still exuded the Hollywood glamour of a much younger star.

The first time Maggie had seen her, Billie was wearing a fur coat and stepping out of a limo that had arrived late to the studio. When an assistant director berated her for wasting their time, Billie's big blue eyes welled up and she cried, "You're . . . you're browbeating me, you are!" Maggie hadn't understood what all the fuss was about, but the man was made to apologize profusely.

How strange it was seeing them huddle together like that, because they weren't Billie and Judy, of course, but Glinda and Dorothy. Maggie felt a sharp pang watching the tinseled-up

Witch comfort the little farmgirl, and she found, surprisingly, that the unkindness she felt toward them wasn't quite pretend.

That morning they'd shot the opening Munchkinland sequence. Maggie watched filming behind camera as Glinda explained to Dorothy that telling the difference between good and bad witches was simple.

"I've never heard of a beautiful witch before," Judy said.

Billie smiled knowingly; her crown glittered. "Only bad witches are ugly."

This was the line that would stick with Maggie in years to come; even after the fame, well after the Academy Awards and all the interviews, the documentaries and the adoring fans. When people came up to her on the street and recited any number of her signature lines, this was the one that always came back to her, and it wasn't even her own.

Only bad witches are ugly.

Because facing off against Glinda and Dorothy felt absurdly real to Maggie, as if she were, in fact, the Wicked Witch of the West. And when she looked down at the green hands gripping her broomstick she felt like the last of an entire race of broccoli-complected people, one that was engaged in a great struggle, with the hideous and deformed on one side, and the harebrained and beautiful on the other.

At the end of the scene, after—"I'll get you my pretty . . . and your little dog, too!"—Maggie laughed and the cackle filled Munchkinland with its murderous glee, every living being left quaking in its wake. The Witch whirled on her heel, color assaulting her on all sides; she hefted her broom high over her head like an Olympic torch, all the way back to her mark. There was a secret elevator in the floor here that dropped her, eclipsed in orange smoke, making for a clean disappearance. Flames burst out immediately after her exit. Like so many of her maleficent ancestors, she was a pyromaniac, this Witch. She liked to throw fireballs at Scarecrows, light matches and pinch the flame between two beany fingers.

The first take of this had gone remarkably well. The director, Victor Fleming, had asked her if she was willing to do the stunt herself so they could get it in one continuous shot. She agreed. Betty Danko, her stand-in, showed Maggie how to bend her knees and brace for the fall to avoid breaking her legs. Billie had asked to be relocated in the scene, claiming her mark, which was a good forty feet away from the trapdoor, was much too hot. Meanwhile, Maggie practiced kicking her cape train behind her and lining her body with the camera, feet planted firmly in the right place. She knew what to expect: the sulfurous smoke enveloping her, the quick mechanical descent that dropped her out under her stomach, heat blasting out in a fiery wave over her head.

Smoke—Fall—Fire. A clean party trick. Movie magic.

But Mr. Fleming wanted several good takes in case the first didn't work, and in the one after lunch the timing had been all wrong: The fire shot too early. So this time Maggie felt a warm flush rising up her neck, a second or two delay in the pattern of her escape so that it was not Smoke—Fall—Fire, but Smoke—*Fire*—Fall. There was a roaring in her ears, a heat so powerful she thought it might melt her, consume her, as if the fire itself had brought to life her beautiful wickedness.

Only bad witches.

◇◇◇

On Friday there's Show & Tell. They're supposed to bring something that tells everyone who they are. Thursday night, after dinner, his parents discuss his options. The boy ignores them, goes to his room, and comes back in his Dorothy costume.

"No," his mother shakes her head. "Absolutely not."

"*Please.*"

They've decided to limit his dress-up time to one hour before bed. Then he has to brush his teeth and put on pajamas. That's the deal. His mother wants to have the outfit dry-cleaned, but he won't let her. It feels different when he plays in it, now that he's started school, and he's afraid that if she washes the tutu, if she replaces the shoes, it will be even *more* different.

"What about the video case?" his father offers as a compromise. He goes to the living room and comes back with it. "See? You can show off the nice cover, with the Emerald City there in the background. You can even tell them how many times you've watched it. How many is that?"

The boy shrugs.

"Like infinity," his sister says.

"It *is* his favorite," his mother admits.

His father nods, looks at him for approval.

"The shoes too?" the boy asks, but he already knows the answer.

The next morning his mother zips the VHS case into the front pocket of his backpack. She hands him his lunchbox. On the way to the car in the driveway, he tells her he left his workbook inside.

"Hurry up," she says and unlocks the front door.

"Straw-for-brains," his sister calls him when he climbs into the back seat. His mom tells her to knock it off. Neither of them notice the extra stuffing in his backpack.

He has it all planned out. The hardest part is the waiting. When the teacher finally tells them to circle up and a flurry of activity fills the room he asks if he can have the bathroom pass, says he has to go real bad. She hands him the wooden stick and tells him to be quick about it. On his way out he snatches his backpack from the hooks by the classroom door.

In the bathroom stall, he changes quickly. The dance costume is ratty and smells a little, but when he pulls it on over his head, he remembers how it once sparkled. He puts on the shoes, heels clicking on white tile when he steps in front of the bathroom sinks.

"Toto," he says to himself in the mirror. "I have a feeling we're not in Kansas anymore!"

Outside the halls are vacant, a long tunnel of white, clocks ticking on the walls. The boy is a splotch of primary color, running his fingers along grooves in the cement bricks, skipping down to his classroom, his arms linked to the air, invisible friends on either side. *Follow, follow, follow . . .*

He uses the extra inches from the heels to peer through the little window in the wooden door, where he can see his classmates sitting pretzel-style inside. A girl stands in the middle of the circle holding a stuffed animal. He presses his nose against the glass.

They can't see him behind the door. *Pay no attention to the man behind the curtain!*

He wants to stand where the girl's standing. He wants to show them he knows all the lines. He can do all the voices. He wants to act it out together: the kids can be the munchkins, and the teacher can play Glinda. He wants them to love him as he loves Dorothy. He'll show them how.

He reaches for the doorknob and lets himself in.

◇◇◇

Judy came to visit Maggie at her house, a few weeks into her recovery. Maggie was grateful to see a familiar face. She propped herself up with pillows, feeling like an invalid grandmother.

"Thank god you're all right!" Judy said, throwing herself across the bed. Maggie shifted painfully beneath the weight of her co-star.

"Oh, did I hurt you?" Judy said. "I'm so sorry. I just . . . I can't believe this happened!"

Maggie had a second-degree burn on her face and a third-degree on her hand. Her doctor said it could have been much worse, had they not gotten her to the studio's First Aid station as fast as they had, because the paint she wore was copper-based, prone to ignite. She remembered having to hold still as her make-up artist swabbed the green off with alcohol. At one point she told him she needed to scream, but he continued rubbing. She didn't scream.

"It's not so bad," Maggie said. "At least there wasn't a stake." This was her default joke, the one she planned to tell reporters in interviews, but there had been none.

Judy shuddered. "Don't say things like that."

Maggie took Judy's hand with her good one, squeezed. "Thank you for coming. It means a lot." Few had visited her. The studio hadn't even offered to give her a ride home after the accident. She'd had a friend pick her up. When her doctor came to the house to check on her, he said Mr. Fleming had been calling him non-stop, but only to find out when she could come back to work.

"Say, how's filming?" Maggie said. "How's it going with my hideous green face out of the picture?" Another failed attempt at light-heartedness. She was beginning to feel like everything she said was a line from a script.

"It's fine. We shot the Emerald City scenes. But everyone misses you."

"Oh, I doubt that. They know who the real star is."

Judy looked down at her lap. "I wish you wouldn't say that."

"And why not?"

Judy shrugged. "I'm not half as pretty as they all think. See these teeth?" And she bared them, not so much a smile as a demonstration. "Capped. This nose? Not mine. Don't even get me started on the rest of my body. They make me take these awful diet vitamins."

"It comes with the territory," Maggie said, touching the bandage wrapping her face.

"Do you know what Mr. Mayer once called me?" Judy said. "I mean, I've heard it lots of ways. My mother used to say I was dowdy, but Mr. Mayer? He said I was a hunchback. A *hunchback!* Sometimes he calls me 'The Voice.' He says, 'The Voice could do that part. She's a farmgirl, not a princess. She's supposed to be plain!'"

"Oh, Judy," Maggie said, and she beckoned her into her arms. "You could never be plain."

"I feel like such a fake," Judy said, sighing. "Even my name is ugly."

"You have a beautiful name."

"It's not my name!" Judy said. "My real name's Frances. Frances Gumm. Frances *Ethel* Gumm. God, it sounds like a *weed.* The Gumm tree."

"Frances is a perfectly—"

"Mr. Fleming slapped me once. It was Mr. Lahr's fault, really. We were filming the part in the woods, the one when we go—*lions, tigers, and bears, oh my!*—and he kept making me laugh. I was supposed to slap his nose and yell at him, but he kept wiggling his tail, and it was so funny! And so I went behind a tree and I said, 'You will not laugh. You will *not* laugh.' But I couldn't help it."

"And so he *hit* you?" Maggie said.

"I hate them," Judy said, crying into Maggie's nightgown. "I hate all of them!"

They sat like that for a while, Maggie stroking her hair. "Let me show you something. Be a dear and bring me that newspaper."

It lay folded on her vanity. Judy retrieved it for her.

On the front page was a glamorous shot of Billie Burke in a pearl necklace and sunglasses. She was laid out on a stretcher being carried into an ambulance by none other than *Misters Victor Fleming and Mervyn LeRoy after Miss Burke sprained her ankle in a terrible acting accident*—or so the caption read. Beneath her elaborate chiffon gown, Billie was seductively barefoot.

"Have you seen this?" Maggie said, holding it up for Judy to see.

"Oh, yes!" Judy said. "It was dreadful. She missed a step and twisted it. Poor Billie!"

Maggie flipped the paper open and read, "'MGM executives report Miss Burke is receiving the best possible medical care and new precautions have been implemented on set.'" She sat the paper back down. "What possible precautions could they take to prevent her own clumsiness?"

"Don't worry," Judy said. "The doctors say she'll be right as rain."

"But don't you see?" Maggie said and Judy's brow crinkled.

How could she explain it? How she had felt picking up the paper two days ago to see the big hoopla over Billie's poor ankle, when here she was, skin charred, and not a note of apology from the studio. How she once snuck out of her tent and into Billie's dressing room and just stood there looking at the pink satin walls, the chaise lounge, the little fur rug, and all of her beautiful pink and blue puffs and perfume bottles, her powders and baby oils, her bowls of peppermints, her closet full of lace. How Hamilton's nanny repeatedly asked if Maggie was feeling well, because she looked a little green, and how the mirror showed she was right: a sickly tinge remained where the paint had soaked into Maggie's skin.

Perhaps it was selfish of her to expect anything different. She shouldn't begrudge Billie or Judy. This was the way this business worked. It was the way the world worked.

"Never mind," Maggie said. "I'm glad she's doing better. I am, too, by the way. My doctor tells me I'll be able to come back to work in a week or two."

"Oh!" Judy sat up and wiped her eyes. "You mean you *will* come back? Even after—"

"Of course I'll come back."

"I just thought . . . I mean, word around the studio is you're going to sue."

"Ha! Don't bet on it. If I sue, I'll never be hired again. They've offered to pay my medical bills and that's fine by me. You can tell them I'll come back under one condition."

"What's that?"

"No more fireworks!"

Judy laughed. "Of course. I'm sure they'll be glad to hear it."

They weren't. Not long after Maggie's return, she was asked to wear a fireproof costume for the skywriting shot. She refused. "I've got a little boy to take care of and I don't intend on jeopardizing my life anymore. You've had all the chances you're going to get with this girl." She even warned her double, Betty Danko, against performing the stunt, but Betty said it was an awful lot of money to turn down. Maggie drove home from the studio, fuming. She was in the house less than an hour before she got the call from the studio that said Betty was in the hospital. The pipe on the end of the broomstick had exploded.

Maggie slammed the phone into its receiver again and again, thinking, *those wicked people.* She sank to the kitchen floor and wept like an old woman. Hamilton crawled into her lap. She told herself she was weeping for her friend Betty Danko and for all the other actors who had suffered the studio's cruelties. But maybe it was more for her own ugliness, a weakness as plain and human as her face. Or for Judy, whose fate she couldn't begin to foretell, who might otherwise have been a happy high school graduate in a simple, white dress.

◇◇◇

He goes to see the revival on campus. The film club hosts a classic movie series every fall, and a girl in his European History class asks if he wants to go that Friday. He doesn't even know what film it is until he sees the Technicolor poster on the tripod outside the auditorium.

When he sees it, he feels a deadbolt turn in him, and he braces himself behind the locked door, as he does when it comes up in conversations with his parents. *Oh, remember when,* they say. *Wasn't it so funny, that time*—like making it into a joke he can be in on, rendering it into family myth, makes it somehow easier than just pretending it never happened.

He's seriously considering bundling up his coat and trudging back to his dorm in the snow when his date shows, in a purple corduroy skirt and peppermint tights, an artistic smatter of freckles dotting her cheeks, two brunette braids defying gravity on either side of her head with a coat hanger.

"Hey, where's your costume?" she says, pointing at a flyer—*FREE admission if you come dressed as your favorite Oz character!*—posted on the theater doors.

"Well, what are you supposed to be?" he says, defensively. "Last I checked Pippi Longstocking wasn't in this movie."

For a second she looks stunned, hurt. Then she reaches into her purse, extracts a giant lollipop with a rainbow swirl. She pinches her nose closed, bobs like an oompa loompa, and sings in falsetto, "We represent the lollipop guild, and in the name of the lollipop *guillld* . . ."

"The lollipop guild is a trio of *male* munchkins," he says. "The female equivalent is the lullaby league. Maybe you meant that one?"

"Wow." She hides the lollipop back in her purse. "You must really like *The Wizard of Oz.*"

"No," he says, startled. "I *hate* it."

"Oh," she takes a step back. "I'm sorry. I thought—"

"I mean," he says. "I don't know. My sister used to watch it, like, all the time."

"Okay." She offers up a helpless shrug. "I mean, if you don't want to."

"It's just," he says, patting the back pockets of his jeans. "I think I forgot my wallet."

"I don't mind buying your ticket," she says. "Since, you know, you didn't get the whole costume memo." Beneath the faux freckles she blushes a little, as if the very idea of dress-up is childish and she wishes she, too, had come in jeans, cash in hand.

"That's okay," he says. "I think I might just head back."

"Wait. I've got you covered." She digs around in her purse again. "Could you hold this a sec?" She hands him the lollipop, then heads to the admissions booth.

While she buys the ticket, he can't help thinking: Whose favorite character is *a munchkin*? He considers faking a headache. But she really is nice—not every girl would offer to buy his ticket. And his father keeps asking him if there are any "prospects" in his classes, like he's panning for gold, and his mother is always oh-so-careful to avoid pronouns when she broaches the subject of dating. At least when they call on Sunday there would be something to report back to them.

"I like the Tin Man, too," she says, as they take their seats. "Those big watery eyes of his. I thought about wrapping myself in foil, but we only had Saran Wrap. What about you? I could see you as . . . the Scarecrow, maybe?"

"I always thought this movie was dumb."

"Oh, right. Your sister. But still. You have to admit, it's a classic."

"It's not even all in black-and-white. *Citizen Kane* is a classic. *This* is a farce."

She slumps a little in her chair. He knows he's blown it, but he doesn't care. He hates her. He hates her fake freckles and her perky hair, how cartoonish it is—like she's being electrocuted over and over. He hates her for asking him here. For trying to make him feel better. For making him feel like he has to have a good time. Who cares if she's nice? Who cares what his parents think? Who cares what the guys in his dorm say?

She doesn't say anything else before the movie starts. Just snacks on the popcorn she bought, even offers him some, but he waves her off.

Then the lights dim, the projector flickers, the MGM lion roars and he's six again.

He hasn't watched the movie in over ten years, and still he knows every line. He braces himself, wanting and not wanting to be captivated all over again, but once the film starts he can't shake how *wrong* it is. The Kansas dialogue too quaint, the Oz sequences too garish, the painted backdrops flat as watercolors, the vaudevillian acting way over-the-top. He hadn't meant what he said about it being a farce, but now he's beginning to believe it. He catches plot holes he'd never considered before: Why *didn't* the Witch deserve her dead sister's shoes? What's the Wizard's motivation in sending Dorothy on an assassination mission? And why did Glinda, that conniving fairy, withhold her knowledge of the ruby slippers' power until the end?

Even reminding himself that the movie was made in 1939, he feels nothing but embarrassment for its makers, and for his enrapt younger self, the boy in red shoes, knocking things over in the basement of his childhood home. He'd been duped! By the time the movie reaches its saccharine conclusion—Dorothy obediently clicking her heels together, waking up surrounded by her loved ones, after a bad dream from a bump on the head—he feels sick. He discovers that the moral of the film is exactly the opposite of what it had always meant to him, a message not of escape or adventure, but of complacency, of not straying, of resigning yourself to a world without color.

"If I ever go looking for my heart's desire again," Dorothy beams from the screen. "I won't look any further than my own backyard. Because if it isn't there, I never really lost it to begin with!"

What nonsensical tripe. What a bunch of baloney. What a wicked *lie.*

On their way out, into the cold, he holds his fists tight inside his pockets.

His date cups her hand to catch a drifting snowflake. She holds it out to him in her palm. "Look," she smiles. "Poppies."

◇◇◇

Three years after the premiere Maggie got a call from the mother of Michael Berman, a boy in the same first-grade class as her son. She'd dropped Hamilton off earlier that day for Michael's sixth birthday party.

"Oh, Maggie," Mrs. Berman said. "I'm so sorry about this. I wasn't thinking."

"Did somebody say something to him? He can be overly sensitive sometimes."

"Oh, no, nothing like that. It's just, well, Michael wanted to put on a film, and he's been absolutely in love with *The Wizard of Oz* lately and so . . ."

"I see," Maggie said.

"I didn't even realize until Hamilton ran out of the room. I'm so sorry."

"Don't worry. I knew this would happen eventually. He hasn't seen the movie yet, but we've talked about it."

They had more than talked about it. Maggie had given him several stills that showed her in full witch garb, green paint and all. Hamilton had been so impressed that he carried them around with him in his backpack and insisted on taking them to school for Show & Tell. He would periodically take the shots out in the grocery store, the barber shop, the park, holding them up to strangers, announcing, "That's my mommy, the Witch!"

"Is he very upset?" Maggie asked Mrs. Berman.

"No. I don't think so. He's in the kitchen eating ice cream. I think it's more that he knows he's not allowed to watch it, than he was upset by what he saw. But maybe you should come get him anyway? Just in case? Again, I'm so sorry about this."

"I'm heading to an audition, but I'll be there as soon as I can. Don't worry. Tell him I say it's okay to watch, as long as he remembers what I said about make-believe."

"Are you sure?"

"He has to grow up sometime."

When she picked him up a few hours later, he had a giant bag of party favors and an enormous grin on his face. He climbed into the back of the car.

"Quite the loot, Ham!" she said.

"Mom," he said after he buckled his seatbelt. "I saw your movie."

"That's great, Dear. Did you like it?"

He sat quietly for a second, thinking. "What did you do with all those men?"

"What men?"

"You know, the ones with the fur hats?"

Maggie hesitated. "Well, honey, those were actors. You know, like how I'm an actress. But it's only pretend, remember? So at the end of the day we all took off our costumes and make-up and went home to our children."

"But what did you do with them?"

"Nothing. They weren't really guards. I'm not really a witch, am I?" But even as she said it, she felt the urge to check her face in the rear-view mirror.

Years later, and still they'll ask her to do the cackle. It's good publicity, but it will wear on Maggie. She'll never return to teaching; the only time she's in schools after Oz is for charity work.

"Please," they plead, up on the stage in the auditorium. Another award, another address for Margaret Hamilton, the Wicked Witch of the West. "Pretty please?"

They want to hear it again, the sound of their childhoods, the one that kept them up late at night, that gave them something to fear other than their parents and teachers, their classmates and friends. The little green woman. Her pointed hat. That hooked nose.

And so she gives it to them. She'll laugh her wicked laugh, and in the silence that follows she'll close her eyes to their frightened faces, waiting for the applause.

◇◇◇

He gets held up at work, so he's late arriving at his sister's house. She's off to some banquet or other and has asked him to babysit. He parks in the drive, hurries up the walk to her front door. He stands on the yellow porch, pressing the doorbell, listening for its distant, tinny ring.

Nobody lets him in. He knocks. Nothing.

He takes out his cell, but the door swings open before he can call—his sister standing there in her elegant skirted suit, tall and regal as a guard in uniform.

"Jesus Christ!" she says. "Come in already. Do I have a sign up somewhere that says knock until the end of time? I'm late enough as is."

"Sorry." He's always respectful of boundaries, perhaps excessively so. He had not thought to try and see if it was unlocked.

Inside, the foyer is dimly lit, awash in green—late afternoon sun filters through the leaves of sycamores that line the house's front bank of windows. He squats down to take off his shoes, a pair of oxblood penny loafers he sets by the front door.

"Don't worry about that," his sister says, gathering her purse from the table by the door. "The house is a mess. Dirt won't hurt it."

"I don't mind. I'm more comfortable in socks anyway."

"Okay, well. She's watching TV. Money for pizza on the counter. Bed by ten. You've got my cell. Thanks so much!" She kisses him quickly on the cheek and is out the door.

He stands on the carpet in his socks, watching her car drive off out the window. In the family room his six-year-old niece sits on the couch, watching TV, eating animal crackers.

"Hello!" he says, a little too brightly.

"Hey," she goes without turning from the screen. On the TV a man in a pink cardigan keeps saying, *and that's the miracle of movie magic!*

He swings his arms a little, glances around the living room awkwardly. Frames on the mantle—his sister has removed all pictures of her ex-husband. DVDs lining bookshelves. Stacks of photo albums in the corner. Somewhere, in an album at his parents' house, there used to be a picture of him in the red shoes. One afternoon, in middle school, he'd come home from school upset, after a kid called him gay. He spent a furious hour flipping through every last album, until he'd found the picture and destroyed it.

"What are you watching?" he asks his niece.

An old woman on the TV announces, "Don't worry, it comes right off, see?" She's been colored with some kind of green paint. She takes a rag and rubs it off her cheek.

"Mr. Rogers," his niece says. "Some lady is showing how to play dress-up."

"Oh my god," he says, and his niece raises an eyebrow in a look uncannily like one of his sister's. "Sorry. But that's her! That's the Wicked Witch of the West."

"This is just like the hat I wore in the film," the woman says on TV. She picks up a pointed, black hat and plops it on her head. "Every morning I had to come into the studio very early so they could turn me into the Witch."

"Who?"

"From *The Wizard of Oz*," he says. "You know . . . *We're off to see the Wizard . . .*"

"Wizards? Like in Harry Potter?"

"What! No. How can you have never seen *The Wizard of Oz?*"

But even as he asks, he knows. She never showed it to her.

He remembers his sister on her wedding day. He'd seen their old babysitter chatting with her at the reception. And even though he knew they weren't talking about him, they were probably just catching up, he couldn't help thinking they were laughing at him, at that summer, at how someone as straitlaced as he had once worn such a ridiculous get-up.

"They don't care," she told him. About their parents. About who he could or could not love. "*I* don't care."

"I know."

"Then what? What is it?"

"I don't know."

He'd brought nobody to the wedding. They all saw. But it was not because he was ashamed. Couldn't they see? He *was* brave enough to love a man. That was easy. And he would try. He would surrender to their image of him—boy in red shoes—to the part he'd denied. But it wouldn't matter. Girlfriends. Boyfriends. With all of them, he closed his eyes to remember how it felt, reaching for the knob outside the classroom door. He'd ask himself: Do I love you? Do I?

The woman on the screen says, "See? There's nothing to be afraid of. It's just make-up. It's make-believe."

"It used to be my favorite movie of all time," he tells his niece.

"Oh," she says.

"Should we watch it?"

"But I want to watch this."

"That's okay." He sits down beside her. "Maybe later." And so they sit together on the couch and watch the lady's transformation, from woman to witch, and back again.

Lucidity

The dream conference is in Room 1237 of the Hyatt Regency in downtown St. Louis. You park the car in a garage, cross the street, and take a glass elevator up. You avoid looking out the window, the Gateway Arch a steel ribbon in the distance. The carpet on the twelfth floor is a pattern of interlocking horseshoes that makes you momentarily dizzy. You don't like heights.

There is no 1237. You search through a labyrinth of halls. But the doors go: 1235, 1236, 1238, 1239. . . . You check the invitation you hold in your hand. You go back, retrace your steps. You come across a door that wasn't there before. A golden plaque on it reads: *Lucidity*.

Along the back wall of the conference room there are velvet-clothed tables laden with coffee and doughnuts. You take a seat.

Not long and the presentation begins. A man walks out and stands at a podium. You can't make out his face. He's talking, but what's he saying? Soon others around you begin to introduce themselves. They are talking about their dreams. They are answering the question: if you could dream anything in the world what would it be? You try hard to think of an answer, but you can't focus. The voices surround you, they sound garbled, they are

64

echoes from the end of a hallway, they are mouths moving behind Plexiglas.

Now they're looking at you. What? You're naked. Are you naked? If you could dream anything . . . *anything?*

The moderator is talking about Reality Checks now. You remember Reality Checks:

STEP FIVE: REALITY CHECKS

1. If you wear glasses, take them off. If you can still see perfectly fine, you are dreaming.

2. If you wear a watch, check the time. Look away. Check the time again. If there's a dramatic discrepancy, you are dreaming.

3. If there is a flat mirror nearby, take a look at your reflection. If there are distortions of any kind, you are dreaming.

4. If there is a light switch, go to it. Turn the lights off. If the lights stay the same, you are dreaming.

5. If there is none of the above at your disposal to check reality, look at your hands.

Across the room you see her. But it's not her. How many times on the street did you glimpse her in a stranger's face? How many times did you see her shoulders, the dip of her neck, leaning over a stroller in the park? How many times have you gone up to a woman in the grocery and scared her with that look of recognition?

She wears the red trench coat you bought her for your tenth anniversary, years ago. She doesn't look a day older than she did then. She's wearing the Gateway Arch on a necklace around her neck. She stands up and walks toward you, smiling, and you see it *is* her. Cassie.

And you think: this. This is what you would dream if you could dream anything. And this makes you . . . Wait. You don't wear glasses or a watch. Where are the light switches? Where are the mirrors? She's almost reached you, and you want her, oh, how you want her, but it's no use, it's only wanting, it's—

You look down and see there are seven fingers on your right hand. You are dreaming. You wake up.

◇◇◇

On your bedside table is your dream journal. You pick it up, flip open to a blank page and stare at it, pen at the ready. Your fridge hums in the dark. The apartment walls constrict. You try to remember, to conjure up something, anything. Nothing.

◇◇◇

The dream conference was in the gymnasium at Jaremy's old middle school. You found the flyer advertising it on a telephone pole outside a bar one night when you were walking home. You tore off the strip of paper with the meeting info and tucked it into the front pocket of your jeans, trying hard not to think of Jare, thinking instead of how it was something funny you might show your friend Cable. You never seriously considered going. How you ended up in the parking lot out front of Jare's school on a Sunday sure beat the hell out of you.

You sat in the driver's seat for a long time, watching the numbers change on the dash. You ran a hand down your face, massaging your eyes with two fingers. You gripped the steering wheel in front of you. Mouth dry. Eventually, you got out of the car.

The gym smelled of floor wax and adolescent B.O. There were about twenty metal folding chairs grouped together at the center where the initials REMS formed the school logo. Standing in line for doughnuts and coffee next to the metal bleachers didn't bring back any fond memories.

You'd always hated school. Couldn't wait to get out of there. You wanted a job *doing something*, out in the world, where life seemed to be moving, continuously, without you—because you were trapped behind a desk for six hours in a concrete-walled classroom that felt like a prison. You took it personally, having to sit and copy words, play number games on scratch paper, forced to listen to talk about ideas that didn't mean anything outside a book.

But Jaremy. Jare. Always your contrarian, your Jare—he'd loved school. Couldn't get enough of it. You could never figure it out, how different your kid was from you. He'd burst into the house after the bus dropped him off, waving workbook pages over his head, chittering like a squirrel, about a documentary on the lost colony of Roanoke, the tiny bones dissected from an owl pellet, so many new equations he'd learned in chemistry! Then it was orchestra and chess team and the A+ society club of academic G.P.A. acceleration. Cassie dragged you to boring ceremony after boring ceremony, Jare awarded a miniature trophy with a plastic chess piece on top, a sew-on patch of musical notes, a tiny gold pin *in the shape of a pencil* for God's sake! Seriously? you thought. These were the medals your son wore "with honor"?

He was a good kid. Too good. Better than you were, sure. Lots. Wonderful potential. At Open House his teachers just *raved*. But while Cassie was enrapt in an environmental-awareness collage Jare made out of recyclable products—aluminum cans, bottle caps left lying around the house—you paid closer attention to the looks the other kids gave your son, to how Jare mostly stared down at the floor, red-faced, shuffling his feet. You knew kids could be mean. You'd used the words yourself in school. Suck-up. Brown-noser. Teacher's pet.

Jare would spend hours in his room working on homework and you'd ask him, isn't it about time to take a break? Don't you want to go outside and have some fun? All work and no play . . .

But it was always: Sorry, Dad. Gotta finish my physics web homework.

Hafta type up this report on the Venus flytrap.

Really need to finish this sugar-cube model of the Great Ziggurat of Ur.

The whatta what of wha?

It's like a pyramid, Dad. Built in Mesopotamia, circa 21 B.C.

Circa? you thought. Just whose kid was this?

Einstein's, Cassie once replied. She was scrambling eggs at the stove. She gave you the look.

Jare sat beside you at the breakfast table; he was reading poetry at that time, not physics. He stuck his head deeper into the textbook, so his nose almost touched the page. That's how you knew he wasn't really reading. His forehead looked red. You hadn't meant to blurt it out.

I have a thing for messy old-man hair, Cassie said. She drifted into monologue, swooning about the kitchen (she made a habit of taking jokes too far): His hair was as white as the chalk that graced the lapels of his jacket. He had a way of clapping his erasers that I just couldn't resist. Oh, Steiny! E really *does* equal MC-Squared. Oh, how your atomic bomb blew my mind!

Ewww, Jare said. Stop. You're going to make me puke.

Yeah, you agreed, nudging your son. Me too. You rolled your eyes. Tell me about it.

Anyway, Jare added. Einstein wasn't directly involved in the Manhattan Project. He only wrote the letter to FDR that started the whole thing. And he took it back later.

That's right, Cassie said, salting the eggs. Your poor, biological father always regretted that. Especially on his deathbed. I hated to see him go. Leaving us with this sad sack to raise you.

You made a mock-offended face. Jare laughed. It felt good. You felt better. Cassie set the plates down on the table. She handed you a fork.

I need a drink, you said.

Coffee, Cassie said. She came back with a mug.

Later, she yelled at you for what you'd said in front of Jare. What could you possibly have been thinking? she asked. How would *you* have felt if your father said that about *you?*

Good, you said. You were drinking a beer on the front stoop, after having mowed the lawn. What? He was a crappy father. Aw, come on, Cass. He knows I didn't mean it.

He cares about what you think of him, she said. Can't you see that?

Of course, you said; and you *did* see. It was all in good fun. In fact, it became a running gag in the family. Like a car game on a road-trip.

Bill Gates, Cassie might say, peeking in on Jare before going to bed. Galileo. Mozart.

Freud, Jare said, smiling up at her from his desk. Ivan Pavlov. B.F. Skinner.

At times the names they ping-ponged back and forth were so obscure it was like they spoke a language that was purely their own.

◇◇◇

There were seven others at the conference. Middle-aged, haggard-looking all. When you took your seat in the sad circle of chairs, you couldn't help but wonder if this was what you too looked like. You found yourself wishing more and more that Cable had agreed to come. You needed someone on the inside of this joke.

Not long and the presentation began. A thin man with a mustache stood up from one of the chairs and introduced himself as Leo Scapes, the founder of *Lucidity* and the Twelve Steps to Lucid Dreaming. He welcomed everyone to the meeting, and asked for introductions, which proceeded with the expected mundanity—my husband recently left me and I'm looking for a way to take back some control in my life . . . When I lost my job last week I thought I'd hit rock bottom . . . I have no time to enjoy myself anymore except maybe in my sleep. So boring that you soon began plotting ways you could escape. You thought about excusing yourself to use the restroom, then slipping out the back. Faking an important call on your cell. But before you could launch yourself into action, they were all looking at you.

Hello, Leo Scapes said warmly. And why are you here today?

You cleared your throat. You took a sip of burnt coffee. I have a sleeping problem, you lied. And I was hoping coming here might help.

Leo Scapes asked what kind of sleeping problem and the rest of them stared enviously at you, like you had a leg-up on them.

Insomnia, you said. Narcolepsy.

They looked at you, incredulous, like: *both*? Leo asked you to explain.

You told them that you have trouble sleeping at night and when you do fall asleep you have trouble staying asleep. Then, during the day, you're so tired you drift off without meaning to.

Well, Leo Scapes said. We're here to help. He retrieved a box from the side of his chair and then passed it around the group. You took out a paper *Lucidity* handbook and a black-and-white speckled composition notebook. These are your dream journals, Leo said. Keep track of them. This is very important. It's the first step of the program!

According to the *Lucidity* manual, this is the first step of the program:

STEP ONE: RECORD YOUR DREAMS

Dream Journal: Keep this with a pen beside your bed at all times. When you awake in the morning or at night do not turn on the light or open your eyes. Hold on to the last image of your dream, then reach over, pick up your dream journal and write down everything you can remember. Make this a habit in your routine. Dream recall must increase before further steps toward *Lucidity* can be achieved.

Leo asked everyone to go around the room and share a dream. It could be a recurring dream, a favorite dream that happened only once, any dream so long as they recalled it vividly. When it was again your turn you told them that you don't remember your dreams.

Ever? Leo Scapes said. Surely not. Surely there's something.

You shook your head, shrugged.

Jare used to dream. He once told you he dreamed in cartoons. Everything was so colorful! he said. There were even colors that didn't exist in the real world.

Don't be smart, you told him. He was interviewing you for his science project.

No, really, he said. Like UV-rays. It looks sort of like indigo, but not.

You remember he had one of those tri-fold standing poster-boards. At the top he'd rainbow Sharpied in bubble letters: "Dreams: Figments of Imagination or AR?" The last couple of letters were squished together. Below that was a sleeping smiley face with a cloud coming out of its head. Cassie helped him with the artwork. She'd always been creative like that. Could draw. Sing. Dance.

What's AR? you asked.

Alternate Reality, he said. Like a parallel universe or something. I would have written it out but we ran out of space.

You shook your head. His projects were always something like that. One year he did "Hypnotism: Self-Trance or Mind Control?" He walked around the house waving that stupid plastic medallion in front of your face for weeks. Another one of his genius ideas was "ESP: Fake Power or Real Brain Wave?" He'd wanted to do "Telekinesis: Mind Moves Matter?" but had abandoned the idea after concentrating on a paperclip for three and half hours with non-conclusive results. This time he was conducting ten case studies, asking friends and family what they dreamed. You were one of his test subjects. Subject #2. Cassie was #1.

Blackness, you said. Or maybe blankness.

Come on, he insisted. Mom did it.

She remembers her dreams. I don't.

Which was not exactly true. Cassie didn't dream. She had nightmares. She used to wake you up in the middle of the night, shaking the bed violently. She was a worrier; she spent so much time being nervous during the day that it carried over into the night. Her worst, most recurring nightmare was of Jaremy trapped in a frozen pond beneath a sheet of ice. She stood on the clear surface above him with an axe in her hand. Although this detail varied. Sometimes it was a shovel. Once, she said, it had been a machete. While Jare froze beneath her feet, his palms banging upward on the under-side of the ice, bubbles escaping from his mouth, she hacked on the lake-top, chipping away, but never fast enough, always failing to break through, watching the life drain from her son's eyes.

She'd told Jaremy none of this. When he interviewed her (you eavesdropped from the hall—Jare insisted that the simultaneous presence of two test subjects during one of the interviews would skew the results, rendering the experiment invalid) she told him she dreamed of lilac fields—of an enormous clearing of purple blossoms. She said she dreamed of Jaremy when he was a baby—of the way the nursery looked and how she rocked him in her arms. She dreamed of getting old in the house you used to live in, and sometimes she dreamed of her teeth falling out.

You couldn't be sure how much of this was true. Perhaps she was merely omitting the bad. But you thought that most likely she had to invent the good, too.

Well, which is it? Jaremy said testily. Blankness or blackness?

You looked at him, tapping his pencil against his yellow legal pad; you knew how frustrated at you he could get for ruining his research, and you loved him for it. No, he wasn't anything like you, and even though that sometimes bothered you, even though you couldn't always understand, you loved Jare for being what you could never be. For how serious he was, your little scientist, your baby Freud; for how little he knew of the world, and how desperately he was hoping to find it out.

◇◇◇

At work the next day you tell Cable about the meeting. The dream journal. All of it.

Sounds like some crazy shit, he says. But you're still going to A.A., right? Your parole officer checks up on that. You can't swap one for the other.

Sure, you say. Sure. Sure.

Cable gives you the once-over, nods. Nailgun, he motions, and you hand it to him. Cable and you work for Coopers Construction Company. You're building houses in a new subdivision called Meadowlark Estates. The clubhouse is recently finished, complete with indoor pool, gym, spa, cocktail bar, and golf course. Cable and you call it "the white picket palace." There's a sign at the front gate that says *Coming Soon!* with a white bird flying over the words.

What's a meadowlark look like anyway? you say, at the concrete mixer. You try to remember if Jare ever did a school project on birds. If Cassie helped with the drawings.

I dunno, but I know it's not that, Cable says.

You know a lot about birds?

No. But I know a dove when I see one and that's a dove. Not a finch. Or whatever.

Meadowlark, you say.

Yeah, Cable says.

Get this, you tell him. At the end of the meeting they made us say this stupid chant.

It's not funny, he says and he stops nailing. You've been out three months and you're acting like these groups are all one big joke. You need the support. You want to risk it?

You don't say anything, just work the mixer. You keep hearing it, over and over, and you want to say it, you want him to hear it and laugh about it with you, but you can tell Cable isn't having any of it. There's a silence, then the nailgun fires a series of staccato beats.

This was the chant you read out of the handbook (from STEP THREE: SHARE AND CARE!) at the end of the meeting:

> May we
>
> Sleep perchance to dream
>
> Dream perchance to wake
>
> Wake perchance to achieve
>
> *Lucidity!*

Well, really you just sort of mumbled it along with the rest of the group while Leo Scapes trilled like a bird, clapping his hands with glee. Beautiful! he said. Wonderful! See you next Sunday. And have a blessed week. Who knows what dreams await you!

Perchance, you mutter now, under your breath. It's a word Jare might have used.

What? Cable says.

Nothing, you shrug, and go back to work.

◇◇◇

STEP TWO: INCREASE YOUR DREAM RECALL

1. Before going to sleep look around your room. Increasing your awareness of your environment before entering a state of sub-consciousness will increase your chances of remembering your dreams.

2. Repeat the *Lucidity* mantra to yourself before falling
   asleep. You might also say aloud: I am going to sleep now.
   I will remember my dreams. I am going to sleep now. I will
   remember my dreams.
3. Set your alarm clock for the middle of the night, around 3
   or 4 AM, to wake yourself in the middle of your sleep cycle.
   Record your dreams. Go back to sleep.

It's obviously not working. You do everything the book
tells you. You sit up in your bed and you examine your crummy
bedroom in your crummy apartment. The plastic Walmart
storage bins with your socks and underwear. The tower of
cardboard boxes in your closet. The forest-green horseshoe
wallpaper. The black mini-fridge. You say the chant so many
times it becomes an endless loop in your head. Without fail,
you jerk awake in the middle of the night, two or three minutes before the alarm you've set is about to go off: 1:58 . . .
3:49 . . . 2:52 . . . You grope for the journal on your bedside table, but it's always the same: cold sweat, tangle of sheets,
and their names.

◇◇◇

The dreams shared at your meetings become more and more vivid
each week. You sit listening to dreams of dancing the tango with
Ricky Martin on *Dancing with the Stars!*, of discovering the lost
city of Atlantis underwater (without any scuba gear at all!), of par-
tying in Vegas and winning over ten billion dollars on slots. Sure,
there are nightmares too, as disturbing as the dreams are enter-
taining. One set in a post-apocalyptic world run by a dictatorship
of mutant spiders. Another a bungee-jumping accident. Montages
of grief and terror and you're jealous of them all. Dream recall has
increased by 80 percent in the group—on average, each *Lucidity*
candidate is happy to report that they lose their dreamscape upon

waking only 1–3 days out of the week, and a few have already achieved optimal dream recall.

Every meeting Leo Scapes saves you for last. While everyone is sharing, they avoid eye contact with you; they feel guilty that you should be excluded, even if it's not really their fault. When the room's attention shifts to you everyone leans forward, thinking: surely this week's the one!

Anything? Leo Scapes asks. Anything at all?

But you can only shrug and say, Sorry guys, not this week. You've considered lying to them. Making something up. They are beginning to get impatient with you, they are beginning to feel you've broken the *Lucidity* Dream-Share Contract. You know what they're thinking. That there's no way you've *never* remembered *a single* dream. That you must be hiding something from them, stockpiling secret hopes, fears, desires. You must be repressed. In denial. You don't really want to get better. You're not even trying. You don't even care.

Which is not true, you want to tell them. It's simply not true.

◇◇◇

Cable and you are at the White Picket Palace looking for bricks. It's ritzy inside: cherry wainscoting, gold door handles, chandeliers, full-length mirrors. You stare down at your work boots, tracking mud across the oriental rug. You follow Cable through the lobby, out to the golf course, where there's a small brick house on the green, a light on in the upstairs window.

You stand on the lawn, leaning against a mailbox. Shapes move behind the curtains. You look up at the stars, then walk over to your car in the driveway, climb in, back out into the street.

You drive for awhile. The headlights aren't working, but you keep going.

Can I lick the stamps? Jare asks in the passenger seat beside you. He's four years old.

Can you drive me to the library first? Jare asks from the back-seat. You turn your head. He's about thirteen. Next to him, an eight-year-old Jare says he has to pee really bad. Between them in a car-seat is baby Jare. He smiles at you.

Buckle up, guys, you say. Let's be safe.

You look into the rear-view mirror to see if they are following your orders and you notice something strange. Around your neck is a piece of silver. A dinner plate? You blink and look again and see that it's actually a giant penny, Abraham Lincoln's profile—stoic as ever.

Also, your nose has been replaced by a sugar cube. You are dreaming. You wake up.

◇◇◇

STEP SEVEN: ACQUIRE A DREAM TOKEN

Choose a small object that has personal meaning to you; it should be very familiar, one you see every day. This can be an article of clothing, jewelry, a photograph, a figurine, whatever you so please. Carry this object around with you. Look at it frequently. Before you go to sleep, hold it in your hand when you repeat the *Lucidity* mantra. When the object turns up in your dream take a close look at it. Something will be different or inexact. Use this replica of your token as a reality check. You are dreaming.

At the next meeting everyone has to share their token. They're pretty predictable objects. A feather. A marble. A pocket-watch. You brought Jare's hypnotism medallion. You dug it out from one of the boxes in your closet. While you're waiting your turn, you slip it off from around your neck, hold it in your hand. You run your fingers over the smooth ridges. Pocket it.

You tell Leo Scapes you forgot your token. The group is dis-appointed, but not surprised.

Originally, you thought of using something of Cassie's—the red paper earrings, her leather bookmark, mementos you've held onto, the detritus of a past life. But you decided against it. She wouldn't want you to. It wouldn't be right.

◇◇◇

Hallelujah! The first *Lucidity* member has had a lucid dream! Space-Dreamer comes bustling into the gym one Saturday to report that yes! Finally! All her work has paid off! Last night she dreamed her typical dream: she was on the moon. She was floating around, minding her own business when for the first time it occurred to her that, hey, wait a minute. She wasn't wearing an astronaut suit. And, hold on just a sec, she took off her bifocals and she could see just fine! She looked at her charm bracelet and saw that it was gold, not silver. She was dreaming! And she didn't wake up!

Instead, she returned to Earth. She flew around her old neighborhood until she found her lousy ex-husband. He was watering the flower beds, like she had always asked him to do and he had never done in real life. She flew right down over him, scooped him up, and gave him a real scare, left him on top of a Chick-fil-A billboard over the highway. Then she had sex with Ricky Martin (who, the group has repeatedly reminded her, is gay) in a cloud for, count'em, *five* straight hours!

Wow, everyone says. That's fantastic! Leo Scapes beams like a proud father.

It was like an RPG! Space-Dreamer says. You know? Like that game Second Life that my son always plays. It's like I'm in complete control! I can do anything!

Wet-Dreamer is next. Two weeks later. He says now he can have any woman he wants, any time he wants her, any way he wants her. He tells you he's had to buy *three* new sets of sheets.

Then it's History-Buff-Dreamer. He comes in bragging about all the celebrities he's met. Paul Revere. Sacagawea. Rosa Parks.

Wish fulfillment, you think. Not long and they'll all have what they want.

You can see that they are beginning to take your lack of progress as a personal offense. They begin badgering you with questions to get to the "root" of the problem. To help you "really let go." At one meeting, while you're in the bathroom, they steal your dream notebook. That's a breach of the *Lucidity* Code of Privacy: Rule #4. You tell them so. You look to Leo Scapes for order. You demand retribution. This is egregious! you say, fist tightening around the hypnotist medallion in your pocket.

Who's Cassie? Leo Scapes replies. Who's Jare?

They look at you, wanting to help. Wanting only for you to let them in, to share your story. And so you tell them. Everything. The accident, the funeral, jail. Except you say it was your narcolepsy that crashed the car. Not you. It was the sleep disorder that killed Jare. You tell them sleep has never been a refuge for you. It is a dark empty space. A black hole. You are so angry, you tell them. All the time, so goddamn angry. And now this. This betrayal of trust. From the *one* group of people you thought you had left. You are deeply hurt. They should be ashamed, you say. Shame on you. Shame on all of you and your stupid dreams!

And so you leave. You leave with the promise of never coming back.

◇◇◇

It's raining. You stand in the parking lot, dripping. You fumble for your car keys, but all you have in your pocket is the medallion. You look again. Did you lose them?

Straight ahead of you there's a woman in a red coat running to her car. She holds a school textbook over her head. Cassie? You ache to follow her, but you can't, you shouldn't, you walk back across the parking lot. Your car's not there anyway. No car is there. The lot is empty.

The rain picks up. You run to take cover inside the giant pyramid next to the school. A sphinx majestically graces the top. Jare waits for you at the entrance. You feel suddenly giddy when you see him. You try to take him into your arms, to dance a little with him, a waltz, but he shoves you away: Get away from me! I hate you! I hate you! Then he's only a pair of glasses on the other side of a downpour. You reach for him, but he's lost in all that water.

Come on! you yell. Please! The pyramid! Hurry!

He's screaming at you from inside the cascade, but you can't make anything out.

Just get in the pyramid, Jare! you shout, latching onto his arm, pulling.

He struggles; you yank harder. Get in now, you say. I mean it.

You're sunk. That's what he's screaming. Like a nailgun: Sunk. Sunk. Sunk.

You try one last time, but his skin is slippery and the pyramid's closing. You think you've lost him, you're sure he'll drown, you tell him to trust you, please, if he'd just trust you and get in.

You sure? he says, sudden clarity in his voice. And before you can answer you're both inside.

As you walk down the tunnel the pounding of the rain recedes. You walk through the garage door and into the kitchen where Cassie is waiting for you, leaning against the counter, talking to herself in a hushed voice. There's a neat row of miniature Gateway Arches sitting in front of her. She looks at you with dark eyes, holds up an Arch.

Where's Jare? you say.

What the fuck is wrong with you? Cassie screams and she throws the Arch at you. It shatters against the cabinets, shards of metal raining down.

I'm sorry? you say, and you laugh. You know you shouldn't, but you can't help it. It's funny.

Cassie holds her head in her hands. You have to stop, she says, calmer now. Please. She walks over to you and puts her hands on either side of your face. Presses them. You have to stop.

What? you say. What is it?

You have to stop dreaming, she says. She takes hold of something flat and round, hanging from your neck. She brings it to her lips and bites into it, chews.

You see then that it's a pancake, hanging from a red cord. You are dreaming. You wake up.

◇◇◇

This time when you wake, your face is wet. It was raining, you think. You remember. It was raining. You go to the trash, where you've discarded your journal. You take a beer from your fridge. You write it down.

◇◇◇

Cable and you stand on the edge of a pit—a future suburban basement. You fiddle with Jare's plastic medallion in your pocket. Cable looks at you, crosses his arms.

A friend of yours stopped by yesterday, he says. Leo. Told me you were pretty upset at your last dream meeting. Everything okay?

Fine. Your lips and gums feel swollen, numbed, like you've recently visited the dentist, that tingling sensation of Novocaine.

He said you told them about Jare, Cable says. That true?

Maybe, you say, tugging at your bottom lip. Where are the mirrors? The light switches?

Cable looks at you funny. He looks funny to you. Distorted. Like a fish in an aquarium. Like a reflection in a carny mirror. Funny . . .

Leo thinks you have narcolepsy, Cable says. That you fell asleep at the wheel. Why would you say that?

True enough, you say and cough.

Hey, Cable says. He yanks you around by your shirt. You been drinking? He shakes you a little. Your head feels heavy on your neck, wobbly.

What the fuck? he says.

Stop it, you tell him. You put your hands over you ears. Stop screaming at me.

Jesus, Cable says. I don't believe this. Cassie was right. And I stood by you. I told her you were going to meetings. I told her— Goddamn it. You fuck. You fucking need help.

Where's she? you hold onto his arm. You know . . . tell me where's she?

I'm calling your sponsor, Cable says. You're lucky it's not your parole officer, you fuck.

You slump to the ground. You're crying. Are you crying?

He's dialing a number now on his cell.

You take the hypnotist prop out of your pocket, hold it in your hand. You look down and see it's a poker chip. Your sobriety chip. The dream token. It changed. Reality check!

Are you dreaming? You're dreaming. And you don't wake up.

So this is what it's like. *Lucidity.* You feel invincible. You can do anything. You can be anything. The world is yours to control.

You walk right up to the side of the giant hole in the ground. You're laughing now. Jare, you say. Cassie. You can get them back. In your dream, he's alive again. In your dream, she still loves you. In your dream, you can fly right to them. You toe the edge of the pit.

Behind you, Cable pauses in his phone conversation. He yells your name.

Next thing you know, his hands are on you and you're lying in the dirt at his feet.

Fucking suicidal! he yells.

I'm sorry, you say. I did it. I killed my son.

Cable kneels in the dirt. He puts his arms around you. You drop the sobriety chip and sob into his chest. Jare's medallion dangles from your neck.

◇◇◇

STEP ELEVEN: CUSTOMIZE YOUR DREAMS

Now that you've honed your meditation skills, you are ready to begin crafting your own individualized dreams. Make a list of things you've always wanted to do, but never could, because of either personal or worldly limitations. Get creative! Once you've entered the lucid dream begin experimenting. Imagine yourself in a zoo. Climb right over the fence that surrounds the animal habitats. Pet a lion, ride a giraffe, swim with the penguins, have fun! Go to Paris, fly to the top of the Eiffel Tower. Be the president, cure cancer, have a vampire love affair! It's all in your grasp now. *Lucidity* awaits you. You're almost there!

Three more months, and now you're standing outside her St. Louis apartment with a bouquet of roses in your hand. You set them on the floor, and bend over, hands on knees, trying to catch your breath after walking up twelve flights of stairs—the elevator out.

Jare wanted to go to college in St. Louis. He'd already been researching the Psychology departments at Wash U. They have a good program, and it's close enough to home, he said. You'd overheard him telling Cassie that he wished he could just skip over high school and go straight to attending university. That's what he always called it: "attending university."

You stand up, fix your tie, pick up the flowers. Breathe. Knock.

You can hear her moving around in there. You imagine her slipping on her shoes, putting on mascara, yanking a brush through her hair. Her last minute prep before answering the door, the frantic grooming you were once so used to.

The chain jangles and the door opens and when she sees your face it's like a cloud passing over the sun. She looks different. Her hair shorter, cut to her chin. A stylish pair of glasses—jade frames—instead of her contacts. You hold out the flowers dumbly.

She stands, braced against the doorway, not taking them. You want her to invite you in so you can talk. So you can *really* talk this time. You want to tell her you're sorry and you want it to matter, you want it to take the place of all the other sorries you've ever been sorry for. You want to explain about the A.A. meetings. About how you haven't had a single sip since that day with Cable. You want to tell her that you visit Jare every week. That every time you go to the cemetery you're looking for a flash of red, hoping she might be there too.

Go away, she says, and she closes the door. It catches your foot.

Cassie, you say. But just her name stops you up. You stand there, caught.

Your foot, she says.

What do you dream about? you ask her. Do you still dream about lilac? Did you ever?

Please go away, she says. You slide your foot out, and, slowly this time, she shuts the door.

◇◇◇

Now you're at the science fair. Rows of poster-boards atop cafeteria tables. Your wife beside you in her red trench coat. Your son is explaining his project to the judges. He gestures to his hypothesis, methodology, results. Someone hands him a blue ribbon.

He turns to you and it's your dimples in his cheeks.

You're a regular Doogie Howser, you tell him.

Bobby Fischer, Jare says.

Haley Joel Osment, Cassie says.

Don't look too closely. There are no mirrors. No light switches. No clocks. When you ruffle his hair make sure not to linger on your hands.

Night Thieves

Lyssa couldn't sleep because she was afraid Jesus might break through her bedroom window and kidnap her. Okay, she knew it wouldn't happen like that, but that's what she kept seeing anyway. A white-robed, bearded man perched in the pine outside her window like a hobo of a sweetheart come to whisk her away from a pair of disapproving parents.

Only it was Heaven they were going to and not some late-night greasy spoon with a jukebox where they could dance the night away. Lyssa was almost eleven and had never even seen a real-life jukebox, much less danced the night away to one. Now she was picturing Jesus doing the Twist, swinging his hips while eating a hamburger, then sucking down a strawberry milkshake. That cheered her up a little. She liked picturing Jesus doing fun things, even if they were fun things she herself wasn't allowed to do. Mostly you just saw Jesus up on a mountain somewhere with a big staff and maybe some lightning flashing behind him to emphasize his points. That was the Jesus she tried to shut out, pulling her pink and white, tulip-patterned bedspread up over her head.

If she was going to be truthful, Lyssa had to admit that what she was really afraid of, even more than being kidnapped by Jesus, was *not* being kidnapped by Jesus. Maybe he'd come for all the others—for her parents and her brother Lee, for Becca May and Pastor Deids, and all the other members of Providence Church in Salva, Texas—and when she woke the next morning everyone she ever loved would be gone, and all that would be left in the world were people who hadn't loved Him enough. Just like she'd seen in the movie.

Earlier that evening, before Lambkins, Lyssa had helped her father, who was the youth minister at Providence, set up the film projector. Her father lugged the dusty monstrosity up from the church basement, delegating her the task of carrying the film itself—that precious 8 m.m. cargo, coiled safe inside what looked like three round cake tins that Lyssa balanced perfectly one atop the other.

Lyssa's father was a slender man with ruddy cheeks and yellow-blonde hair that he gelled in a wavy style, which Lyssa thought made him look a bit like Hermey, the dentist-elf from Rudolph the Red-Nosed Reindeer. He was tall, but not very strong, and not used to lifting heavy equipment like the film projector, so by the time he had carried it up the stairs, through the entryway, down the nave, and to the front of the chapel, he had crumpled to the floor beneath the weight of the load and had to set it down before heaving it up onto the altar.

Lyssa held the film tins in front of her, careful not to get dust on her green velvet dress. She lingered in the doorway to the chapel to admire the stained glass behind the altar. This was the one place she could make out every frame. Her eyes danced outward from the red heart on the giant cross in the center panel, along the blue and green and yellow rays that emanated to the farthest corners of the sanctuary. She felt then what she could never feel on Sunday morning, no matter how hard she tried. During services, when she had to sit in the front pew with her family or stand and sing with the choir, her faith always felt like a performance for the congregation. But when she was alone with her father in the great mystery of the church, when colored lights from the windows shone on her face and arms, making a pretty rippling effect, as they did now with the late afternoon sun setting outside, she felt, with almost a violent urgency, the desire to kick off her shoes and go running down the center aisle, sliding across the waxed floor in her frictionless tights. She imagined Jesus sliding beside her in His socks and underwear, like Tom Cruise in *Risky Business*—a movie her parents still didn't know she'd watched with Becca May. It was in moments like these that she truly knew Jesus loved her with all His heart, and that she loved Him too—if not as much as she loved her father and her mother and Lee, then definitely at least fourth best.

Her father would not have liked that. Lyssa knew his order was: Jesus first, then her mom, Lee, and her. "How do you have J.O.Y in your life?" he'd ask the Lambkins. "By putting Jesus first, Others second, and Yourself last!" Lyssa knew Jesus was supposed to be her number one, too.

Once she'd tried to find out Lee's order. They were doing Bible study at the kitchen table, having finished Math—Pre-Algebra for Lyssa, Calculus for Lee. This week's Bible study was on the temptation of Christ. Lee read aloud from Matthew, Chapter Four, in which *the devil taketh him up into the holy city, and setteth him on a pinnacle of the temple* . . .

While Lyssa listened, she kept thinking about that scene in *Spiderman* in which Spiderman had to choose whether to save Mary Jane or a tram car full of children after the Green Goblin dropped them off a bridge. When Spiderman saved both, Becca May scoffed and said, "What a cop-out! That is *so* Hollywood. In real life you'd totally have to choose. Those kids would be fish-food." Lyssa didn't know why that had upset her so much. *Of course he saved both,* she wanted to say. *How could he not?* But she soon realized Becca May was right. After all, that was the whole point of a choice, wasn't it? You couldn't have it both ways.

So she interrupted Lee's reading and asked, "If Jesus was hanging off the pinnacle of the temple and I was hanging off the pinnacle of the temple, and you could only save one of us, who would you save?"

Questions like these were not uncommon between them; they'd always had a weakness for brainteasers. Since they were both homeschooled, they often entertained themselves by trying to stump the other with trick questions:

If a man's peacock lays an egg in his neighbor's yard, who owns the egg?

If an electric train is going 80 mph, how fast is the smoke blowing out behind it?

Which is heavier, a pound of bricks or a pound of feathers?

Lee tapped his pencil against his chin. "What do you mean, hanging off?" It was his usual strategy: poking around for more information before guessing. A premature guess could make you look really stupid. Even more than coming up with the right answer, this was the object of the game: to not look stupid.

"I don't know." Lyssa shrugged. "You know, if we fall, we're dead."

"But that doesn't even make sense. Are you even listening? *He shall give his angels charge . . . and in their hands they shall bear thee up.* If Jesus fell, they would catch Him."

"Well, I know *that*," Lyssa said, blushing a little. "I just meant, you know, *hypothetically.*" This was one of Lee's favorite words; he prided himself on his ability to stretch his imagination.

"Okay, then. Explain it to me."

"I just meant, if Jesus wasn't God. If He was human and you had to choose."

"But He wouldn't cast himself down. He resists Satan's temptations. How would He be hanging off the pinnacle? Did Satan push Him or something?"

"Who cares! You have to choose: Him or me? That's all that matters."

"Okay, but it's a tricky question. Because if Jesus wants me to sacrifice Him to save you, He'd really be safe all along, so it wouldn't even be a sacrifice. Or maybe it's a test, like Abraham's, and I should let you fall because really the angels will catch you?"

Lyssa sighed. "Forget it, okay?"

"Hey, come on, Lys. You don't have to get so upset about it."

She knew he was right. It was a dumb question. So why did her eyes have to sting so dang much? Why did she have to shut herself up in her dang room, pretending to read a dang book the rest of the afternoon so he wouldn't see? And why couldn't she keep from cursing in her dang head? What was wrong with her? If she had asked her father the question he would have answered Jesus without hesitating. If she had asked her mother she would have said it wasn't polite to ask such questions, that life was rarely either/or, it just wasn't that simple.

Later that night, after she was in bed, Lee slid a folded piece of paper under the door between their rooms. They did this often; she had an entire shoebox of notes stashed under her bed. But this time she wouldn't read it. She wouldn't even look at it. She'd tear it in half and slip it back under the door and then see what he had to say about it.

I'd choose you, it said in his leftward-slanting scrawl. She wished she could believe him.

◇◇◇

"How bout it, Lys?" her father said once he'd set up the portable movie screen and tripod. She came down the aisle in the church to meet him, holding the film tins before her as if she were in a processional. She laid them out—one, two, three—beside the projector.

"How's it work?" she asked, peering into the lens.

He opened the tins to reveal the reels and showed her how to thread them into the projector, how the tape spun and the glass eye magnified the image. Lyssa absorbed the lesson with the same reverence she felt during the sermons her father gave to the youth group. His hands moved with the conviction of his speech, in fast deft gestures. His voice was high-pitched, as if he had inhaled helium as a child and his vocal cords had been permanently damaged. As with his sermons, when he came to the part of the demonstration in which he was most passionate, his throat tightened, his Adam's apple bobbed like a yo-yo, and his voice leapt higher, not louder, jumping an octave into a strained falsetto. It was a sound more akin to the chicken squawks that left the mouths of startled adolescents than the deep bellow of Pastor Deids that commanded the attention of the congregation every Sunday. This was believed to be the reason he had never been promoted to a more respectable position than youth minister—at least, according to Lyssa's mother and her mother's friends.

"Why don't you get the lights and we'll try her out?" he said, unwinding an extension cord.

Lyssa forgot herself a moment, half dashing to the back of the church before her father told her to slow down. She reached up and flicked the switches one by one (there were seven of them), then walked (slowly) back to her father. He plugged the projector into the cord, pointed out the power button, and gave her the honors.

There was the dull clanking of metal on metal—a sharp rat-a-tat-tat!—then the whisper and flick of film unspooling. Numbers counted backward (6 . . . 5 . . . 4 . . .), Lyssa lipped them silently in anticipation (3 . . . 2 . . . 1 . . .), and the show began.

The movie was an educational film from 1972 called *A Thief in the Night*. Her father screened it every year for the Lambkins right before summer vacation, but this was the first time Lyssa got to watch. Her mother disapproved of the film; she'd told Lyssa's father it gave the kids nightmares. There had been complaints among the congregation. Nothing too serious, nothing brought directly to Pastor Deid's attention. The women talked amongst themselves about it, mothers who saw their children grow quieter at the dinner table, who lay down with them in bed to help them fall asleep.

"It gives them something to think about now that they're distracted without school," Lyssa's father told her mother. "They need a lasting impression in the weeks before Noah's Adventure." He meant the Vacation Bible School that Providence led, the Monday through Friday church retreat (sing-a-longs, tie-dye T-shirts, prayer collages) that didn't begin until mid-July.

"It scares them," her mother said.

"There's nothing to be scared of if they accept Jesus into their hearts."

"They're children," she insisted. "Good grief, Simon. You know First Corinthian doesn't show that film to kids under fifteen. And it's eighteen for UCC, unless the parents give permission."

"Okay," he said. "I hear you. But it's a good film. There's nothing in it you can't find in the Bible, for crying out loud." That always ended the discussion. Lyssa's mother knew: you can't out-talk Scripture.

Lyssa's father shut the projector off, and they went to set up the snack tables. Soon the early Lambkins arrived, mini-vans pulling up in the parking lot. Kids and teenagers untangled limbs from back seats. The meeting began with the opening prayer and greeting, followed by the group song, "Jesus Loves You, This I Know," complete with hand motions. Then Lyssa's father began his sermon on the Second Coming.

"In the Rapture only the Chosen will Ascend," he said. "That means each and every one of you needs to take a good look in your heart and decide for yourselves: will you be among the few Jesus takes with Him or one of the many left behind?"

Lyssa sat alone in the front pew, trying her hardest to do what her father said. She closed her eyes and rested a hand lightly on

her chest—which, unlike Becca May's, was still flat as any boy's—
and she tried to find Jesus there. She envisioned the four-cham-
bered organ beating beneath her palm. Her homeschool group
had recently taken a field trip to the Museum of Natural Science
in Houston, where there was a giant replica of a heart that you
could walk into and explore. Inside, the walls of the right atrium
and ventricle were painted blue to signify de-oxygenated blood
pathways, and the left were painted red. There were also noise
machines that mimicked the *lub-dub, lub-dub* sounds of the muscle moving and light projectors that sent disco-like shards of light
shimmering along the floor like blood cells.

Lyssa's father had declined the museum's offer of a tour guide,
opting to lead the group through the displays himself. In the
giant heart he gathered the homeschoolers around him while a
museum guide leading the group next to them lectured about the
pulmonary valve.

"Take a gander," Lyssa's father told them. He whistled loud
enough to draw a look from the guide. "Lordy! How on Earth
could an organ as complex as this be created by *chance?*"

This was the heart Lyssa imagined Jesus standing in, holding
His arms out to her. Maybe if she went to Him, if she really felt
Him there, it would be like blood changing, blue to red.

But she was too distracted—by the itchy lace collar of her
green velvet dress, by the film projector and the stained glass
windows, by the murmur of the kids shifting in the seats behind
her. Many were older than her (technically), but they weren't
half as mature. Her mother liked to joke and say that Lyssa was
born an eighty-year-old woman. She was a severe-looking girl
with dramatic cheek bones and dark, check-marked eyebrows
that stood out on her forehead. She didn't like being around
kids her own age, or even those slightly older than her (except
for Lee), preferring the company of adults, her father mainly,
and a few of the older parishioners, who would sneak her extra

doughnuts after services. She wished Lee were here, instead of at some dumb car show with Chase Garrett. Lee didn't even like cars.

Her father was talking again. His voice was like a fly in the room, a shrill, piercing drone. Because he was rarely given the opportunity to preach in front of an adult audience, he made use of his time in front of the youth, continuing to make his points well after he'd lost their attention.

After they sang again they took a break to get snacks from the tables set up in the church entryway. Lyssa and her father had laid out bowls of popcorn and pretzels and red paper cups filled with fruit punch and lemonade. Lyssa wanted to snatch a handful of potato chips and maybe say hi to Becca May before they started the movie, but her father told her to wait. After he had led the other Lambkins out to the food, he came back in from the atrium and shut the doors so it was only he and Lyssa in the chapel. He brought out from behind the altar a large cardboard box. Lyssa thought it might be more parts for the film, but when her father opened it she saw it was filled with old clothes.

"Here," her father said. He took a pile into his arms, then dropped a pair of hand-me-down jeans on the floor. "Scatter these around."

"What? Why?"

"You know, like when your room's dirty."

Lyssa looked at him. Her room was rarely, if ever, dirty.

"I mean, like Lee's room. When Mom has to get him to pick up his clothes."

He was tossing garments all around now. Winter jackets slung over the backs of pews. Piles of T-shirts discarded up and down the aisle. Lyssa just stood there.

"Well, what are you waiting for?" he said. He shoved a tangle of gaudy sweatshirts at her, then went back to flinging pairs of basketball shorts. Lyssa sat down on the floor and unraveled the knotted sleeves. She folded the clothes, then lined them up in neat piles on the pews.

"What are you doing?" her father said. "They're supposed to be *messy*. Just throw them on the floor."

"But why?"

"So it looks like they've been Taken."

Lyssa was confused, but she did as her father asked. She unfolded the sweatshirts, then meticulously arranged them on the floor so they looked like they'd been dropped there. As she worked, she kept thinking, taken by whom? The clothes had been donated by church members for the poor and homeless, but they hadn't been given out to anyone. They'd been stored in a box in the church basement for who knows how long.

"All right, that should do it," her father said, and he hid the empty cardboard box back behind the altar. Lyssa almost asked if maybe she could get some punch now that they were done, but her father was already hurrying to let the Lambkins back in. He skipped down the aisle he was so excited to show the kids what they'd done.

At first they were as perplexed as Lyssa. A few of the older kids made jokes.

"Looks like a tornado went through a strip mall."

"Where are all the naked people hiding?"

Lyssa's father ignored them. "Imagine," he said, rainbowing his hands. "That everyone you ever loved disappeared. Imagine coming into church one day and seeing nothing but a room full of empty clothes. Where have they gone?"

"To Heaven!" It was a little girl in a pink tutu—either Soshanna or Deedree, Lyssa wasn't sure. "Jesus took 'em up."

"Yes," Lyssa's father said. "They've been Taken. They've all been Taken. And now you're all alone. Because you didn't love Jesus with all your heart."

In the silence that followed Lyssa couldn't supress a shiver. She looked around the chapel at the clothes strewn about, only this time they weren't holey tank tops or mothball-ridden khakis. Instead she saw Mrs. Krazinsky's floral print dress and gaudy pink pearls. Mr. Hughs's flannel shirt and his leather boots with the horse-shoes on the toe. The Disney Princess costumes Soshanna and Deedree always wore—blue and yellow, Cinderella and Snow White—their plastic tiaras topping the satin piles like cake decorations. Lyssa's eyes wandered up to the altar where the robes and sashes of the choir would be all in a line, as if discarded on the floor of a changing room. There was a whine from the back of the chapel. One of the younger kids was frightened.

"But I do love Him!" It was Soshanna. Lyssa was sure this time. "I do I do I do!"

"All right!" Lyssa's father laughed. He clapped his hands. "That's what I like to hear. We all need to love Jesus as much as Deedree does."

"You know what *I* think we should do?" Becca May stood in the back. She was a pretty girl with light blonde hair. She was in the same homeschool group as Lyssa. "*I* think we should all pray together and ask Jesus to come into our hearts right now. Just in case there are any *unsaved sinners* in the room."

"I think that's a great idea, Becca!" her father said.

"May," Becca May corrected. She said it in a mockingly high-pitched tone. "Becca *May*."

"All right, everybody," he said. "Let's all pray with Becca May!"

Lyssa squeezed her eyes tight at first, but eventually she couldn't keep from peeking. Most of the other kids had their heads bowed low, but Becca May was looking smack dab at her, playing with the miniature gold cross that hung between her collar bones. Lyssa glanced away.

"Oh, Jesus, we just pray that you can come into our hearts and bless us," Lyssa's father was saying. His eyes were closed and he was rocking on his heels, his voice climbing the register. With every new rung of intensity, Lyssa was afraid his Adam's apple might pop like a balloon.

She wouldn't look at Becca May. She wouldn't.

As soon as Becca May had Lyssa's full attention, she performed an exaggerated, slow-motion eye roll. Then she mouthed the words, *Pee-wee Herman*. It was the name some of the older kids called her father. Lyssa didn't know what it meant, except that it had Pee in it, which said enough.

She'd first heard this after her father forfeited her solo in "Amazing Grace" to Becca May. Sometimes Lyssa's father stood in for Providence's music minister, Mrs. Miller, who was also Becca May's mother. She was always calling in sick last minute. Lyssa's father said this was because she had a "weak constitution," but her mother said that was just an excuse for her to spend Sunday mornings at the spa, which Mrs. Miller insistently called a "homeopathic remedy." Lyssa's parents fought over it, because her father didn't get paid any extra for putting together all the music, lyrics, and equipment, or for leading the choir, and the church kept paying Mrs. Miller's full salary so she could cover her "medical bills."

Three Sundays ago, Becca May and her mother showed up at Providence an hour before the service while the choir was going through their last practice run. Mid-song, Mrs. Miller tapped Lyssa's father with a pink, acrylic fingernail attached to the end of a long, bronzed finger and told him she had it from here.

"Really, I don't mind," Lyssa's father said, but Mrs. Miller just smiled at him.

"Lyssa can sing the harmony," she told him, as if this had been his motivation all along: the chance to put his daughter in the spotlight.

But Lyssa was relieved to give up the solo. She'd only agreed to it because she knew her father would be disappointed otherwise. So she was surprised by how she felt when Becca May stepped forward in front of the congregation and let forth a sound more beautiful than any Lyssa was capable of making. Just from the looks on the faces in the front pew, she knew how her family would compliment Becca May afterward. Her mother used the word *divine*. Lee, whom Lyssa had suspected had been in love with Becca May for years now, could only nod and grin like a dope. Her father, however, took Becca May's hand, held it to his heart, and said, "Can you feel that? He's in there. I felt Him when you sang. Thank you for that."

Before Lyssa could stop herself, she imagined the worst possible fate for Becca May. She willed herself to think something hateful so that she wouldn't have to see her father standing there, loving Becca May like he had never loved her, knowing she would have to swallow her pride and parrot her father, telling her best friend—who she didn't even like, not even a little—that she thought her song was beautiful.

But she couldn't think of anything terrible—or her conscience wouldn't let her—not while she mouthed the words to the harmony, not after the service while her family was mooning over Becca May, not even the next day when the homeschoolers broke for lunch and Becca May whispered in her ear, "Your dad gives me the creeps. He's like in love with me or something. And he sounds like Pee-wee Herman. It's totally obnoxious."

Only later, in dreams, did Lyssa's brain provide her with the image of a freak puncture wound to Becca May's gullet, golden shrapnel from her exploding cross pendant, lodged in her windpipe so that she could never talk—much less sing—again.

But when Lyssa awoke, she felt so guilty she'd had to close her eyes and invent a miracle cure: a syringe filled with purple liquid that was injected into the white bandage around Becca

May's throat. And when that didn't work, she imagined a voice-box transplant, which still didn't quite make up for her guilt, since Becca May would be stuck with Lyssa's nasally voice, the one she had inherited from her father, and Lyssa would be for-ever mute, although it might be nice to have an excuse not to say things she didn't really mean anymore, like she had to do that day in church.

"Lyssa?" her father said after he'd returned Becca May's hand to her. "Aren't you going to tell Becca what you thought of her singing?"

"It was pretty," she said, wanting to say *okay*, but not going so far as *beautiful*, and secretly proud of herself for it.

◇◇◇

The movie screening was saved for last. After the Lambkins were done praying—Becca May's cry of Amen! ringing out over the rest—Lyssa's father finally signaled for the lights, and beckoned Lyssa forward to start the reel. They took their seats together in the front pew, and Lyssa felt much safer with her father by her side. Even though she'd liked helping him set up the movie, she was scared to be watching it for real. Lee had prepared her.

"It's like a horror movie," he said. "Except without all the gore," which relieved Lyssa a little, until he added, "And God's the serial killer."

A Thief in the Night opened with a black screen and a loud ticking sound. Lyssa felt that ticking in her breastbone. It was like standing in a shop filled with clocks all in time together—already her heart was pounding. A blurred image appeared, clarifying into a yellow alarm clock next to a radio. A voice on the radio clicked on and began discussing an event that had occurred the night prior, strange disappearances. A woman sat up alone in bed. She rubbed sleep from her eyes. Her hand paused on her face, trem-bling out of nightmare. She spoke a name, Jim? Jim?

Lyssa tightened like a band. Without knowing it, she drew in close to her father until her leg was pressed right against his. Lee had been right. This *was* scary.

Beneath the ticking there was another sound now, this one softer, as if coming from a distance, and just as Lyssa was aware of it, the ticking seemed to fade into the background, and this new sound, a buzzing, filled the space it had left behind. The woman rose from the bed. She was wearing a gaudy pink nightgown. Her hair was long and wavy in the style of the time.

She was kind of pretty, Lyssa thought. Although part of her allure was a fabrication, a disguise. It was the haziness of the film, its melancholic feel; it was a fondness for the past that her mother called *nostalgia*. She said it in such a way that Lyssa knew it wasn't a good thing.

She thought of watching old movies with Becca May, who sometimes invited her to stay over after they had class in the Millers' living room. The actors were all young and beautiful, so glamorous that Lyssa often floated in a daze for hours after the movie—as if life itself had been reinvented into a movie, the world made universally kinder and infinitely more interesting.

Becca May, however, would prop up her feet, pop a kernel of popcorn into her mouth, gesture at the screen, and say, "Wow. And to think they're all dead now." A group of new characters would walk in the door and she would point and say, "Dead. Dead. Dead. Hey! You're dead, too." It was a kind of revenge: to be living when they, the celebrities of a previous generation, were no longer. But Lyssa didn't always see it that way. They were in Heaven. They were with Jesus, and so it didn't matter that they were dead and gone.

The woman on the screen was only half as pretty as those old actresses. She looked a little haggard, making her way down the hall toward that incessant buzzing. It was coming from the bathroom and, though she had never seen one in real life, Lyssa couldn't help picturing a chainsaw.

As soon as the actress threw the door open, the camera cut into a close up of an old-time electric razor, plugged into the wall, rattling around in the sink.

The voice on the radio made sense now. Jim had been Taken. He was one of the Chosen. And this woman, this girl, poor little Patty, as Lyssa would come to know her in the next hour, and think of her in the resulting days, was not.

Patty screamed like she'd been stabbed.

Lyssa flinched next to her father and he took her hand. The rowdiness among the Lambkins sitting behind them had finally quieted down. Lyssa felt a warmness spreading in her lap that she thought was blood. Was she hurt? Had she been the one stabbed? Was that scream coming out her own open mouth? She leaned over to tell her father, but stopped when she realized what it really was that was staining her tights, darkening the green of her dress, and then she was too embarrassed to say anything. Too embarrassed even to go to the bathroom and clean herself off.

Instead she sat and endured it, the puddle of urine cooling in her lap, slowly drying as the film spun on its wheel and the movie played on, Lyssa too afraid to move, praying hard to Jesus to please Take her and Take her now.

◇◇◇

After the movie, Lyssa washed up in the church bathroom. Her father had to take home several stray Lambkins whose parents hadn't come to pick them up. Lyssa was grateful for the other kids in the van. Her father kept asking questions about the film and she didn't feel much like talking. She was afraid they could still smell pee on her.

When they finally arrived home, Lyssa's mother was curled up on the couch under an afghan, watching a news program about an astronomical phenomenon that was supposed to take place that night: a lunar eclipse. As soon as they were in the house, Lyssa went straight to hug her. She crawled into her lap, even though it made her feel a little childish.

"Someone's affectionate tonight," her mother laughed and kissed her on the head. "Was it the movie?" she said, and Lyssa fought back tears. "Did it scare you?"

Her father was unlacing his shoes in the armchair beside them. Lyssa shook her head. She nestled deeper into the dish-soapy scent of her mother's nightgown. She tried to focus on the newsman, who kept blabbing on about the moon.

"Simon," her mother said. "I told you she wasn't ready. You know she's sensitive."

"Aw, don't start. She learned a lot tonight. You should have seen her. Helping the old man out. What a champ."

The newsman, who had grown a full beard in seconds and was now Jesus, said, "This only occurs a handful of times every century, so you don't want to miss out!"

"We really reached them, Sarah. You should have seen them, the way their faces lit up. I mean, *good-night*, Little Deedree. Can you believe it? She's got spunk, that one. Just like Lyssa. She's gonna be a real firecracker. I can already tell."

"You don't have to scare them to teach them, Simon."

"Lyssa's not scared, now are you, Hon?"

"Repent!" Jesus was saying on the TV, jabbing a finger through the screen. "Repent, Lyssandra Marie Darby. I have seen the truth inside your heart and grace does not lie therein."

Before Lyssa could answer either Jesus or her father, the front door opened and Lee came in. Headlights flashed across the living room window as his ride took off down the street. As soon as she saw him, Lyssa knew something was wrong. His face looked smudged and his eyes sunken, but he forced a smile and neither of her parents seemed to notice.

"How was the show?" their father said. He always had to drag Lee to car shows; Lyssa was more of the auto aficionado between the two of them. Lee drove a Dodge Ram, but she doubted he even knew that. Their parents had bought it for him for his six-teenth birthday. He'd had it three months now and still whenever someone asked what he drove, he'd answer, "a green truck." So they were all surprised when he begged their father to let him skip Lambkins just this once, so he could go with Chase Garrett to a show in Houston.

"It was okay," Lee said. He shrugged. "Kind of tired, though. I think I'll hit the hay."

"Well, wait a minute, what did you see?"

"Cars," Lee said, heading down the hall. The door to his room closed without a click.

"Oh, leave him be, Simon," her mother said as he left the room. "Let him sulk."

"The end is nigh," Jesus said, adjusting the microphone clipped to his lapel. "The time of judgment draws forth. You are not pure of spirit, Lyssa Marie. Let me heal you."

There were no locks in the house, but her father banged on Lee's door anyway, waiting for him to open it. Lyssa couldn't hear exactly what he was saying, his voice was too high, but she was sure it was the lecture on honoring thy father.

"Lyssa," her mother said, holding her in her arms. "Please. Say something, Sweet."

"The stars shall fall from heaven," Jesus said. His face now filled the entire screen. "The moon shall not give her light. Be ready, Lyssa. Be ready."

◇◇◇

In her bedroom that night, Lyssa pressed her face into her pillow. After Jesus did the Twist, she made Him do the Mashed Potato, the Macarena, and the Funky Chicken, but eventually the novelty of the dances wore off. She gave up waiting for Lee's response to her note (*You OK?*), and snuck into his room to see for herself.

His bedside light was on and he was sprawled on top of the covers, fully clothed, staring up at a water stain on the ceiling with his arms tight across his chest. She didn't say anything. She just sat pretzel-style at the base of the bed next to his feet, and looked up at the same patch of ceiling.

"Any idea how fast a Laburgunny can go from zero to sixty?" he said finally.

"Lamborghini," she corrected him, and immediately hated herself for it.

"Right. Whatever. Under three seconds. Chase told me that tonight."

"I didn't know the Garretts had a Lamborghini," Lyssa said.

"They don't. It was at the show."

"What color was it?"

"Canary yellow."

Lyssa laughed. That was just like Lee. *Canary* yellow. She could see it.

"What?" he said. "You think that's funny?"

"No. I guess not."

"Oh, ha ha. That's so funny. Lee doesn't know anything about cars. Ha ha. What a pussy."

Lyssa had never heard that word before, but she liked it even less than Pee-Wee Herman. Why was he so mad at her? What did she do wrong this time? Why did she have to mess everything up so dang much?

"Okay," she said. "Sorry."

"You don't know anything, do you? You just follow Dad around like he's the Second Goddamn Coming, don't you?"

Lyssa's mouth went dry. She looked back at the water mark, which gaped at her like an angry mouth. She could hear Jesus's voice on the TV inside her head: Repent, repent, repent.

"Why don't you go pray for a better brother?" Lee said. "Isn't that what you want?"

She couldn't stop thinking of her question about the pinnacle of the temple. She imagined herself on trial in front of Providence's congregation and her father asking her for the hundredth time, Lee or Jesus? Jesus or Lee? She'd probably say what her father expected her to say. But, secretly, she wouldn't have hesitated. She pictured herself reaching over the side of the temple's roof, gripping her brother's arm, pulling him to safety. That's what she wanted to tell Lee. That's what she wanted to share with him, that image in her head: the two of them, standing atop the temple, looking out at the setting sun, Jesus plummeting far below, the echo of His cry unheard, His landing sending up a cartoon cloud of dust.

"Go on, I said!" Lee was shouting. "Go cry to Jesus, but leave me out of it."

Her face was hot, but she wasn't crying. She went back to her room and sat for a while on the bed. Then she knelt down beside it, but she couldn't pray. She just couldn't. She got back in the covers and looked at the ceiling. Who was she supposed to talk to if she couldn't talk to Lee, or to her parents, or even Jesus? She pulled the bedspread up again, closed her eyes, and waited for the voice from the TV to tell her what to do, but it didn't come. It didn't come.

◇◇◇

In her dream, Lyssa stands on the front lawn in her nightgown. The grass beneath her feet as dry as any summer. The pines along the side of the house browned and brittled in the heat. The stars sown above in the great firmament, slivers of seeds in the night sky.

The woodpile's burning. A bonfire in the sideyard. Her father chops logs on a block—each stroke making a loud ch-tick!

ch-tick! ch-tick!—then he tosses the splintered wood, piece by piece, into the blaze. Lee's on the porch swing, swaying back and forth, a Bible in his lap. Her mother's at the mailbox at the end of their drive. She shuts the lid with a snap, then waves at Lyssa, letters clutched in her hand.

Her family's not alone outside the house tonight. All down the street, Lyssa can see neighbors, homeschoolers, and church-goers, all of them, out on their lawns: the Ryles and their six kids, Mrs. Krazinsky and her little dog, Pastor Deids and his wife, Becca May and her parents, the Garrett boys, Mr. Hughs, Soshanna and Deedree. They huddle in groups, talking animatedly, waving their hands, crying, embracing, pointing excitedly up at the stars.

The sky's tearing—it makes a loud buzzing noise like a zip-per. Seeds sprout, spreading their silver roots in the black soil overhead, growing like lightning, fracturing every which way. A strange pressure fills Lyssa's ears and all the sounds of the ticking and buzzing, the shouting and barking and weeping are forced out of her head.

Then feet leave the ground: Pastor Deids rising majesti-cally overhead. Becca May floating upward with supreme grace. Soshanna and Deedree twirling together like lit sparklers.

Lyssa's mother is running up the driveway, trying to get to her when she is suddenly ripped from the ground, letters scat-tering, her housedress blowing up as if in a gust, her pale legs dangling like two branches stripped from a birch. Lee goes next. He stands on the Bible, balancing it like a hoverboard beneath his feet. Her father, following close behind, extends the axe down to Lyssa, blade first, and she tries to leap up and take hold of it, but she can't. She'll cut herself.

She falls back as others flock over her. Holes explode in the ground all around her and out come body parts—solitary legs and arms, livers and kidneys, eyeballs and ears—floating above her as if suspended in a gelatinous substance. Muscles flex, fingers clutch, nerves quiver. Somewhere in the distance she hears the faint muffle of a trumpet, a shout. Then she, too, begins to rise.

Not far behind, Lyssa struggles to catch up, but it soon becomes clear to her that she is not flying, or even swimming, through the air, that she has no control over the speed of her ascent. Far below, she can make out the entire town, receding into darkness. Above her, roots and sprouts are tangling together; there's more light than dark left in the sky. A field is growing, rows of silver wheat. When the neighbors who were taken first, the tiny specks way above her, touch the light they disappear; or, perhaps, they become the light. Eventually, her mother reaches the light and is gone. Then so does Lee and her father. The organs that touch the light knit together before vanishing.

The light is almost blinding now. Lyssa can make out nothing, but a dark smudge. It looks like a human heart. She focuses on it until it clarifies: It's Jesus's head. He is the Light.

As soon as she realizes this, her head bangs against something hard, like glass. Her body tries to keep rising, but there it is again, some glass barrier, between her and the Light.

He smiles at her. Then laughs at her. He shakes His head. The glass barrier, the dome, whatever it is, lowers, sinking her down. She cannot pass. She will not be Taken.

Then whatever has held her up until that moment leaves her. The sky darkens once more and she falls back to the Earth, where no one she has ever loved remains.

◇◇◇

The house was deathly quiet when Lyssa awoke. She was cold and she was terrified, but she got out of bed immediately and went to Lee's room. She didn't care if he was mad at her. She didn't care if he hated her. She needed to see him tangled in his sheets. She needed to feel his breath against her hand. She needed to touch him to be sure he was still there.

But he wasn't. The bed was empty.

Lyssa went across the hall to her parent's room. They had to be in their bed. She had to see them. Their chests rising in their sleep. Her father's mussed-up hair on the pillow. Her mother's sleep mask askew on her forehead.

But they weren't there either.

It had happened. In her sleep, it had happened. They were gone, all of them, and they were never coming back. Outside her parents' window, the moon darkened as the Earth moved between it and the sun. She could not watch. She climbed into their great bed and pulled the covers up so she could surround herself in their scent.

If only her dream had ended sooner, she might have wrapped her arms around her mother when she'd tried to wake her to come see the eclipse.

If only she had gone over to the window and seen the three of them, standing together on the front lawn, heads bent back, watching the Earth's shadow steal light from the sky.

If only she had loved Him more than she had loved them, then maybe she could have kept them a little longer.

Merlin Lives Next Door

A week after I move in he comes over with a plate of macaroons and a fifth of Scotch. I can tell he wants me to ask, so I do, and he says it's more like being unstuck from time than living it backwards. At first I don't believe him, just think he's read too much Vonnegut, but then he sneezes and flies over the porch railing and into last Saturday when I was doing some landscaping.

As I watch him disappear through a tear in the spacetime continuum, I remember him *oof!*-ing into the hedges three days ago, snapping off several already-trimmed branches. (I had to re-clip the entire row.) He looked like some strange overgrown bird, flapping around in that ridiculous cloak of his, the long white beard he wears à la Walt Whitman all tangled in the hydrangeas. I stopped the mower (locking the wheels so it wouldn't slide out of line) and yelled at him to get off my lawn before he did any more damage.

He didn't bother with introductions once he'd extracted himself. Just walked right up to me, combing stray leaves out of his hair, and said, "Well, I hope you at least caught the Scotch." He mistook my look of confusion for condescension. "I mean 'catch,' " he said. "No, 'will catch.' 'Will have caught.'

Well, whichever!" Then he stormed across the property line to his brick hovel, leaving me to wonder how he knew I was such a strict grammarian.

I mulled it over later, searching several handbooks, finally concluding that, given all times exist simultaneously for someone of his condition, the tense he'd been grasping for was the present progressive, i.e. "are catching."

Unfortunately, I don't. The Scotch was, is, *will* never be caught. It shatters on the porch planks before I can even feign a grab. Frick. I get the broom.

◇◇◇

When he comes back over that evening, looking somehow younger, beard more salt-and-pepper than gray, I'm in the middle of alphabetizing my library. I apologize for yelling at him, and for the Scotch. He accepts ungraciously, entering the house uninvited with a six-pack of Newcastle, grumbling that we'll have to "make do." He rummages through my silverware drawer until he locates my bottle opener, and I try hard not to think about the spoons I'd arranged by size: tea, table, soup, ladle. He suggests the porch, and though I motion toward the boxes of books, making some socially appropriate hint about how I still have a lot of unpacking to do, I find myself—inexplicably—in a rocker watching daylight wane and suburban kids chase each other around the court on roller blades with glow-in-the-dark wheels. Merlin clinks his bottle against mine, makes some cheery remark about life. Then he "catches me up" on neighborhood gossip.

Marty Pendrake's boys, twin terrors who torture squirrels in their garage, are destined to be serial killers. Mr. Galwin likes to tan naked in his backyard. The glint you'll see over the fence is from the sheet of aluminum foil he bakes on. Oddly enough, he'll die of bone, not skin, cancer. The newlyweds with the weird

Dutch (or is it Swedish?) names—Trieste and Leopold?—have sex on their deck at 10:30 every night. It's routine. He huffs and huffs like a water-logged dragon, but he won't keep you up for long. Can't keep *much* up for long, for that matter! Ha ha ha! Oh, and don't be fooled by Mrs. LeFeigh, the pretty brunette widow who lives on the corner. Might be nice to look at, but trust me, keep your distance, because I'm telling you, that woman's a straight-up *witch*.

"Oh, really?" I say, thinking: *what are the odds?* I haven't been paying much attention until now. I find myself longing to sort U—mostly Updike, organized sequentially by publication date, not alphabetically by title—but I'm intrigued that "Merl," as he likes to be called, has some vague romantic interest in this Mrs. LeFeigh (*"Vivienne,"* he slips and calls her once). I suspect he's warning me off out of self-interest, not neighborly duty, but I'm fine with respecting the boundaries of his secret affections. They do, after all, have something in common.

"Well, that's a shame," I say, taking a swig from my beer, trying to sound light-hearted, "because I was a real fan of *Bewitched.*"

He looks at me like I'm an idiot.

"I was speaking figuratively, Geoff. I meant she's a bitch. Jesus Christ! How many of us do you think there are?"

I apologize, not meaning to have offended him or his kind. I see the best thing here is to come clean and tell him I've never actually met a magician before, don't know much about them really, and could he be so kind as to cure me of my ignorance?

"Wizard," he says. "I don't pull rabbits out of top hats. I don't know any card *tricks.*" He spits the last word at me and I say I guess I deserved that. We stare out at the constellations of green luminescence, roller blades whirling at street-level. I yearn for copyright pages.

"It's nice having another bachelor nearby," I say finally, to break the silence.

"What are you? Some kind of pedophile that needs to blend in?"

That's it. I'm getting up the courage to order him to get off my property I'm so angry, but then he tells me to take a chill pill and lights a cigarette.

There's something off about the way he smokes. It's backward: he takes a drag on the air, inhaling the smoke, then exhales into the cigarette so the ash near the end turns back into paper, crisp, unblemished, white. I can only speculate as to which law of thermodynamics this defies.

"Seriously though," he says. "Why no Mrs? Or would it be a Mister? I don't judge. I've spent plenty of time in Ancient Greece. But how old are you anyway? Or are you divorced?"

"I'm not. And I'm only thirty-six."

"Thirty-six! In another life you'd have a dozen children by now. And you don't even own a dog for godsake."

"Neither do you."

"Yeah, well. I can't. Who'd feed it while I'm on extended leave in the Sixth Century?"

"I don't know. I guess I could."

"Really? You'd do that?"

"Maybe. I mean, if it didn't interfere too much. I like my life to be—"

"Lonely?" Merl says.

"Uncomplicated."

"Bah! No such thing."

He looks at me then, his eye so calculating I can't help but imagine what has been projected onto that chronologically enhanced retina. I envision glossy photographs from the *History of the World* series that resides on my top shelf. Medieval courts decorated with suits of armor and elaborate tapestries. Women in corsets walking the decks of steamships. Battlefields, eclipses, the Magna Carta, maps of the Lewis and

Clark Expedition, French guillotines, the Egyptian pyramids, Beatles lunchboxes.

What wisdom comes with having witnessed so many epochs of civilization? What terrible knowledge must he bear? I feel a panic then, an episode coming on, and it's like the converging of a timeline, like everything that's happened—*everything*—all forty-eight volumes worth of history, has led up to this moment, has been building to now, when he tells me what he knows. But I'm not sure I want to know. I *don't* want to know. I don't.

But he only sighs. "Everybody has somebody," he says, gazing up at the stars.

I tell him it's late. I think he should go.

"Aw, but it's only . . ." he rolls back the sleeve of his cloak, revealing an assortment of odd-looking watches. The bands travel up the length of his entire arm. There are a few with straight-forward faces, a silver Timex for one, but there's also a miniature sundial, an hourglass, a water clock, and numerous contraptions fashioned out of gears and pendulums, rubber bands and duct tape. He taps one with a glowing digital face: ". . . nine o'clock."

"Sorry," I say, collecting his empties. I stand by the front door.

"Well, alrighty then," he says, hefting himself out of the rocker. He shakes my hand. "Nice meeting you, Geoff. Don't be a stranger now. Toodle-loo!"

I flinch, thinking this some kind of incantation, expecting him to burst like a firecracker or turn into an owl or something, but all he does is saunter down the brick stairs with a resounding belch, leaving the cigarette he's un-smoked in my sweaty palm.

◇◇◇

Although he doesn't come around for nearly a week, Merl's all I hear about. The only thing more ubiquitous than Welcome-to-the-Block committees around here is wizardly scandal.

The neighbors always find a way to ring my bell at the most inopportune time. I'll be midway through tough copy or a stubborn fact-check, colored pencil in hand, and there they'll be, peering through the front windows—calling "yoo-hoo!"—rife with marshmallow-topped casseroles and strong opinions about necromancy.

I try to be polite. I do. I stand there, nodding, and count to a hundred while they complain about how *some people* foretell the BINGO numbers at the Pimberly Nursing Home right on the money, but always seem to draw blanks when it comes to the Jackpot Lotto. Or how a certain curmudgeon (not naming names) refuses to magic up a few anthropomorphic talking bunnies in tartan vests for the annual Easter pageant. (What about the children? they say. Don't they deserve a tea party with a cute egg-laying, pocket-watch-carrying cottontail to celebrate the resurrection of the Lord Our Savior?) Or, god forbid, they go into the Book Club Incident.

Apparently, when Merl first moved in he joined every single neighborhood "activities group." Your typical small town fare. Speed Walking. Euchre. Mini-Van Drag Racing. I've been told he was notoriously good at Underwater Tai Chi. At first the neighbors were unnerved by Merl's hyperactive involvement, but eventually they warmed to him, like a kooky grandfather or an adopted expat from Pimberly's. The women enjoyed his insight on cosmetic herbs and potions, the fountain of youth, the elixir of life, etc. The men were particularly fond of his collection of swords and battle axes, as well as the competitive feats of strength he came up with at potluck suppers. It was not until the disastrous Book Club Incident that his reputation went awry.

No one remembers how the argument started, but the end result was Merl got outrageously angry and turned Lance Dulack into an urn. But it was a nice urn, decorated with an animated scene of the Fourth of July, families on blankets in a field, eating corndogs and watching fireworks go off in the background. The police were called, but that led to a lot of awkward standing around. There was nothing they could do since there was no blood or anything. They did rope off the urn with yellow caution tape, but Mrs. Pendrake took it home after they left.

Merl has never been welcome at another community activity. The neighborhood even formed a new club, the "Warlocks Are Radical Terrorists!" group, or W.A.R.T., to promote anti-sorcery bigotry. They hand me a chartreuse flyer and ask me to join.

"Not to be too PC or anything," I say, "but the term for magic-users is 'wizard,' not 'warlock,' which is derogatory in nature."

Their eyes slit and they snatch the flyer back. They call me a Gandalf-Groper and say I should be careful who I cozy up to on this street. Then they make a homophobic joke about wands and tell me to enjoy the sweet potato pie, which I throw out.

◇◇◇

I'm rolling pennies for the bank, each pile of 100 sorted by year, when Merl shows up. He stands on the front stoop calling, "Hey stranger! Lend me a hand, would you?" I expect he needs help lifting a birdbath or maybe an armoire, but when I come out he thrusts a bottle of calamine lotion at me. Drops his cloak right on my front stoop. He stands there in his Harry Potter boxer shorts, a pattern of little golden snitches against a sky blue background, begging me to "lather up" his back. I see then what I missed before, that his skin is covered in red spots, and his chest and neck already wear a pink crust.

"Please," he says hopping up and down. "You have to itch 'em for me! *Itch* 'em!"

I really don't want to, but I can tell he's in pain so I pour out a handful of the chalky substance and begin to rub it onto his speckled spine. He sighs with relief. I turn my head away, and there on the sidewalk are two boys on bicycles, a jogger, and a mail-woman. Oh god. Merl waves.

"It's 'scratch,'" I say. "Not 'itch.' You don't 'itch' an itch. You scratch it."

He taps his nose. "You've obviously never had timepox."

I leap back, drop the bottle. "What's that? Like chickenpox?"

"Don't worry. It's not contagious," he bends down and picks up the bottle. "Just another symptom of my condition. You gotta scratch 'em to make 'em itch."

"But then why do you scratch them to begin with?"

He looks at me, dumbfounded. "Why wouldn't you?"

I've no answer for such illogic so I go back inside and wash my hands. When I come out again the spectators are gone, but Merl's seated himself in a rocker, still practically nude. He asks if I have any Scotch. I tell him no. I try to be blunt this time. I'm busy. He's interrupting my household errands allotment. Could he please just leave me alone?

"Your what?"

"My household errands allotment." I list off the to-dos on my fingers. Three o'clock: Make a deposit at the bank. Three-thirty: Stop by the grocery. Mail out a manuscript before the post office closes at five. Hair-cut at five-thirty. Laundry and closet organization from six to eight. Stir fry for dinner. Maybe read a book for an hour or so, then bed around eleven.

"Well, aren't you a busy bee?"

"I'm sorry, but there's really no flexibility for socializing." I'm trying not to look at the patches of gray hair on his chest. On the arm without the watches he has a spiderweb tattoo.

"Should I come back and make an appointment?" he says.

I can't tell if he's being facetious, so I go in and get my schedule book. It's reassuring in my hands, this small leather-bound book, each task plotted out in neat calendar boxes, time delineated by my handwriting to achieve the maximum efficiency potential in a twenty-four-hour period.

I open it up and show him the week, booked full.

"I bet you were one of those kids who always asked for *extra* homework," he says. "Come on. Let's play hooky." He twists open a beer—where did those come from?—and holds it out.

"I don't *do* hooky," I say.

Merl frowns. A speech is coming, I can tell. I brace myself for some elderly wisdom. He says, don't I ever get sick of segmenting every second of every day into a pie graph? Haven't I ever wanted to just sit and do nothing for an afternoon? Do I even own a TV?

"Of course I do," I lie.

"Well, alrighty then." He thrusts the beer into my hand and I sit. Then he throws my schedule book into the front yard. I let out an embarrassing little yelp as it lands in the hydrangeas, but when I start to rise out of my chair he shoots me a look that says don't-you-dare.

I don't think it's a spell, at least it doesn't *feel* like a spell, but I keep thinking of the Book Club Incident and I can't move. It's like Merl's cast some Muscle Paralysis Curse, if such a thing exists, and there's nothing I can do but sit there and endure his naked company until the sun goes down. He talks about jousting tournaments and he talks about pub-crawling with Shakespeare. He talks about the Hindenberg. What. A. *Tragedy*. He goes on and on about how swell a guy JFK was. Eventually, I can't take it anymore and I blurt—"Did you really turn Lance Dulack into an urn?"

"Ah." Merl nods. "That. It was an accident. He was sleeping with Gwen and Marty found out. Tensions were high, there was a big fight, and somehow I got between them."

"So . . . why didn't you change him back?"

"Wish I could."

"You mean, you can't?"

Merl shakes his head and it's the saddest thing. "Lance shouldn't have done that to Marty. Gwen, too. Some people. They don't know what they've got. But still. I'd take it back if I could."

"Clearly there's a lot about magic I don't understand," I say.

Merl chuckles—or tries to. "Hell, there's a lot about magic *I* don't understand."

I say, "So that's why Mrs. Pendrake wheels that thing around at night." She's put the urn into a little red wagon and planted a eucalyptus tree in it; I've seen her watering it with gin.

"Enough already," Merl says. He lights a cigarette, then asks about my job. I scoff, but he pretends to be interested in copy. Ha! I tell him it doesn't compare to hunting wild turkey with Squanto or building Stonehenge, but he's actually encouraging about it.

So I tell him. I tell him that it's really an underappreciated art form. I say, don't you hate when you're reading a book that's been labored over by an author, read and re-read by an agent, meticulously edited by an editor, printed by a publisher, sold on the mass market, purchased by you for $19.95 at your local bookstore and there!—right there!—on page 59 is the word "throguh" or "aobut" or, most commonly, "hte"? Don't you shudder with revulsion when you come across the wrong there/their/they're in text that masquerades as quality literature? Don't you think, by God! Somebody should have caught this—hundreds, literally *hundreds*, of eyes must have looked over this manuscript, over draft after draft after draft, and not a single one of them caught the extra period in this ellipsis. . . . .

"No," Merl says. "I don't."

"Well, I do. For sure. There's not a book of my copy that has a single typo. Not a single space or comma out of place."

"Impressive," Merl says, and even though I know he's just humoring me, it feels good to talk about it. He tells me he was once friends with William Caxton, the English printer, during a time when orthography wasn't standardized and true could be spelled trewe, truye, or chroo.

"How awful," I say, envisioning a broken alphabet. "How primitive."

"Your Chronocentrism is showing," Merl says. "He was quite progressive for his time."

"Really? How so?"

This is how I sacrifice a $28 deposit at the bank, a stocked fridge, and peace of mind for Merl's friendship. I lie awake in bed that night and I turn over and over, thinking how terrifying it must be to have no stable footing in time, to bound back and forth from century to century with the ease of walking in and out of a room, with no control over when you end up. I'm so disturbed by this that I rise and go to my closet where I line up my loafers two inches apart. I take solace in the evenly spaced indentations on the ruler, but I can't get his last words out of my mind: Merl, gazing up at the night sky, just before he vanished with a hacking cough, his glass shattering on the planks after he'd raised it to toast the stars and sighed, "Ah. To my old familiars."

There's a crowd of Merlins barbequing in front of his hovel when I come home from the post office a few days later. They spill over from his lawn onto mine, holding hot dogs and burgers, digging into platefuls of pasta salad with plastic silverware, looking like a giant family reunion. At first I don't know what I'm seeing. A teen with a droll little stache tips his pointed hat to me when I pull into the drive. There's a group of nearly identical-looking middle-aged men standing in a circle by my hydrangeas; their beer bellies are in various stages of development, like male pregnancies, but all share the same dark brows, heavy beards. A few of them have toddlers strapped to their hips, the same plump two-year-old with wide, perceptive eyes.

Across the street, the neighbors have gathered on the corner, whispering, and gesturing angrily at the spectacle. They pace back and forth, arms crossed over their chests. Several of them have cell phones out like they're *this close* to calling the police.

They yell at me when I get out of my car: *Sorcerer-Sympathizer!*

The older Merlins, those who resemble the Merl I know, sit in lawn chairs around a circular picnic table, watching the little-kid Merlins chase each other with sticks. Because I don't know which one to address, I glance back and forth between them when I demand to know what's going on.

"Just keeping myself company," one of the Merls says and the others laugh.

"Oh, that's good. That's really good. I'm going to have to use that," another says.

"You will," the first answers with a knowing smile.

"Who's responsible for this!" I shout.

"He is!" they say, pointing to themselves.

I shake my head, slap a beer out of the closest one's hand. "Which one of you is Merl?"

"We all are," they reply in sync. It's like a nightmare in a hall of mirrors.

"But how—" and then I understand. I close my eyes and see a photo album filled with snapshots of Merl: Merl in a crib, Merl on a bike, Merl blowing out the candles on a cake, Merl graduating from magic school. It makes me light-headed, and then the Merls disappear, fading out of the photographs like they're developing backwards, leaving behind the crib, the bike, the cake, empty rooms and empty memories, out of place, out of time.

◇◇◇

When I come around there are four blurry Merlins staring down at me with identical expressions of concern. The panic starts to rise again until my eyes clear and the out-of-focus replicas converge into one familiar middle-aged Merl.

"Upsy daisy, Geoff." He helps me to my feet and over to the nearest lawn chair. Pulls a cup of tea out of his sleeve and holds it out to me. "Got a little discombobulated there, didn't you?"

"Sorry." I look out at the yard, empty, littered with party trash. Across the street, the neighborhood protesters have disbanded. "Where did they go?"

"Home. Oh, where did *I* go? Who knows? Somewhere in time. I very rarely get to visit my selves like that. Once a millennium or so. It's an anomaly. You should be excited you got to see it."

"Forgive me if I'm not thrilled." I rub the back of my head, stare down at a discarded cob of corn. He urges me to drink the tea. I take it from him, blow at the steam, and sip. "I'm sorry. Sometimes I have these . . ."

"Episodes?" Merl nods, pulling up the chair next to me. "I know. You told me. Or you will. Don't worry about it."

"I just need things to be in a certain order, or else it bothers me."

"Sure, sure. I have triggers, too. Stress. Loud noises. A hiccup. And then I'm gone, forward or back. But you learn to live with it. You cope. You rely on yourselves."

I tell him I know the feeling. I've sacrificed a lot to prevent my panic attacks. It feels good to have something in common, something shared between us, even if it has to be this.

"Come on, Geoff," he scoffs. "It's not exactly the same."

"I know. I can't imagine how weird it is. I just meant I can relate a little."

"Oh? Can you? Because your life seems pretty damn stable to me. Let me show you something." He rolls up his sleeve, holds out his right arm. I see what I missed before: from afar his tattoo looks like a web, but up close it turns out to be an elaborate time-line extending from the top of Merl's shoulder down to the tip of his middle finger.

"In the next second I could trip into any of these times." He traces the line with the pointer finger of his left hand. "I've tried to keep track of where I've been in case I go back, but the longest I've ever stayed in one time consecutively is nine months."

I can't help myself: "Is that why you call the stars your familiars?"

He takes so long to answer I can't tell if he heard the question. He's wearing hearing aids.

"Do me a favor, Geoff. One day you'll notice my lawn getting shaggy, my mail piling up. Sell my house. Keep the money. Don't wait for me. Could be a day, a decade, forever."

He scans his forearm for a second, as if looking for a vein, then puts his finger down on today's date where it has *Quantum Entanglement Picnic* and my address.

"I've been looking forward to this day for a long time."

When I lean in further, curious, Merl snatches his arm back, covering it with his sleeve. He says he can see that I'm okay. He apologizes again for his selves, mutters some hokum pokum so the trash disappears from my lawn, and retreats to his own property.

But he's too late. I've already seen what he was trying to hide. *October 13, 1971: Geoffrey Nolava.* Inked over his liver spots. The date of my birth.

◇◇◇

That night, after he's left, I can't stop thinking about the date on his arm—so permanent, so personal, so stalker creepy. So I investigate. I get out every photo album, every yearbook, every box of mementos I've ever owned. Fortunately, I never throw anything away. I keep it all in air-tight plastic bins, labeled by year, organized chronologically in the attic over my garage. I lay everything out on the floor across my living room: a map of my life. I try to look with an objective eye, but after a few hours I do exactly what I warn myself against: I get nostalgic.

Once I get to my senior year of high school I find myself fixating on this one picture of Mallory St. Thomas, my prom date. She's standing by the punch bowl in her puffy periwinkle dress, the DJ mixing in the background behind her. I haven't seen or heard from Mallory in years, but for some reason I can't stop looking at the photo. Mallory wasn't popular, but she was kind and quiet and she'd said yes when I asked her and I was grateful. I might not have noticed her myself had I not caught her smelling books in between the shelves at the back of the library.

I was planning to skip prom (even then I had bad social anxiety), but that changed the moment I caught Mallory with her nose between the pages of an Ursula Le Guin novel. It was a habit of Mallory's that drove me absolutely insane. She'd walk up to a shelf, pluck a book, open to a random page, and smell it. And this wasn't some measly sniff I'm talking about. She didn't *waft* the scent with her hand like they taught us to do in chemistry class. Mallory would stick her nose all the way into the book's spine and inhale deeply. I was so immediately aroused by this, that when she looked up and caught me gawking at her I couldn't stop myself, I couldn't think, I didn't know what to do, and so I blurted out the question as if it had been my intention all along. She looked at me, perplexed. For a second I was scared she might ask what I was doing lurking behind an upside-down copy of *The Silmarillion*, spying on her secret book-smelling.

But then she said yes.

What?

I said yes, she said, and then she walked over to me, took the copy of Tolkien out of my hand and held it up to my nose. Go on, she said. All I really got out of it was dust and book glue, but when I opened my eyes I said *wow* with what I hoped to be a stunned, philosophical look. It occurred to me that I might kiss her then, boldly, right over the columns of elvish translation she held between us, but I didn't. I couldn't. I didn't know how. She smiled demurely, closed the book, and then moved on to Terry Pratchett.

Terry . . . Why is that name familiar? Did we go to school with a Terry? Was he the DJ in the photo? Wait. I look again and this time I recognize him, the guy playing music behind Mallory and the punch bowl: it's Merlin.

He isn't dressed like Merl, but it's him all right. This was the eighties, remember. And when it comes to the fashion of the times, Merl's dressed to a T: a cross between Miami Vice, MJ's Thriller, and Top-Gun (apparently he'd done his research): preppy designer jacket, aviator glasses, white fingerless gloves, long pony-tail pulled back with a purple scrunchie. None of the mish-mash matches. It's as if he's tried to incorporate every clothing trend of the decade into his ensemble in order to blend in. He's clean shaven, mid-twenties, and I wouldn't have recognized him had it not been for the teen with the stache I glimpsed earlier on my front lawn.

I can't believe it. I'm holding the photo in my hand and I still can't believe it.

Merl was the DJ at my high school prom. He played "Every Little Thing She Does Is Magic" seventeen times. We all just thought he was obsessed with Sting.

Now that I've found him, he starts popping up everywhere. On a family vacation in Florida: he's the cabana boy handing my mother a strawberry daiquiri. At the nursing home where I used to volunteer for community service hours: playing chess with an orderly. Another at my college graduation—there, right there, hovering in the background like a lost grandpa. By this time I've started circling his face with a red sharpie wherever I can find it. It becomes a bizarre game of *Where's Waldo?*—Christmases, weddings, first days of school, new cars, publishing parties, field trips, funerals. There's a Halloween picture in which he's bending over, dropping a handful of candy corn into my pillowcase, and— no way, no fricking way!—he's actually dressed as a wizard! His beard's fake, tied behind his ears like a department store Santa Claus. The robe he wears doesn't compare to his cloak: it's cheap, dark blue with little silver stars, obviously from a costume shop. But still. Unmistakable. The irony was wasted on my seven-year-old self.

By the end of the search I've collected over eighty photographs. Only one conclusion can be drawn: Merl is a lifestalker. And I am his subject.

◇◇◇

I plan a speech about privacy. I rehearse an interrogation. But Merl doesn't come over the next day. Or the next. I suspect he's avoiding me until I notice the pile of newspapers on his front stoop. So I go over and knock on his door. Nobody answers. I peek through the front windows. Nothing.

I'd ask the neighbors, but after the Quantum Entanglement Picnic, W.A.R.T. started a petition that, if passed, would require all "practitioners of magical arts" to register officially with the government. I've seen leaflets and I don't want to offend the supporters.

Thankfully, Merl turns up on my porch a week later. He's even younger than before—my age, mid-thirties, mahogany beard, no glasses or hearing aids. He drops a piece of pumice into my hand. Souvenir, he says. From a very unpleasant (and lonely) holiday in Precambria—the result of a prolonged bout of coughing. I'm surprised by how relieved I am to see him. I invite him in for a drink, forgetting all about my autobiographical investigation until he sees it, taped up all along the living room wall with bits of red string, like I'd seen once in a detective movie.

"Hmm . . ." Merl combs his fingers through his facial hair, examining a photo of himself in the hospital waiting room on the day I was born. "Research?"

"Oh, right." I'm vaguely embarrassed. My accusations deflate. All I can come up with is: "What the frick, Merl?"

"Would you believe me if I told you that my obligatory duties in my role as tutor-slash-royal advisor-slash-guardian angel to the King of the Britons, once named Arthur, now reincarnate in the body of one Geoffrey Nolava, twenty-first century copy editor, extend to the body in which his soul has transmigrated, from epoch to epoch, on into perpetuity, etc. etc.?"

"Um, no."

"Well, it was worth a shot. Now about that drink?"

"I'm serious, Merl. Why are you in all these pictures?"

He sighs, shrugs. "I don't understand it myself."

"So, what? You're *accidentally* stalking me?"

"It's not stalking if it's unintentional."

"Semantics, Merl!"

"Look, I don't know what to tell you. Our lives intersect randomly. The universe doles me out how it pleases." He's digging in the liquor cabinet now. "Somehow, by the logistics of some unfathomable karmic physics equation, it makes me gravitate toward certain people." He takes out the gin, goes to get the glasses. "You're not the only one, you know. Don't get cocky. You're not that special."

Still, I can't keep myself from asking, "Why me?"

"How do I know?" He clinks ice into the glasses. Pours for both of us. Stirs. "Maybe the galaxy sensed some kind of imbalance, like a human black hole, and it figured that the self-designated misanthrope could use a friend. A mentor. Yours truly."

"A *human black hole?* What does that even mean?"

"Come on, Geoff. You're nearly forty and all you have to live for is grammar errors."

"*Are* grammar—" I say, and he smirks. "It's my job, okay?"

"If it's just your job, then why do you barely leave the house? Tell me something. When did you last go on a date?" He holds out my drink.

I snatch it out of his hand and dump it down the sink. "That's personal, all right?"

"Let me ask you something," he says, chewing on a lime. But I don't want him to. I wash out my glass, let the water run. "Why didn't you kiss Mallory St. Thomas?"

"What!" I remember something then: I forgot to buy her a corsage, had to make her one out of tinfoil. The only origami I could do was a crane. She wore a tinfoil crane to the prom.

"I know you wanted to. You had chances. In the library. After the prom. Why didn't you kiss her?"

I try to remember what Mr. Ambrose, the high school librarian, looked like. He used to wear jeans that were too tight and ties that were too skinny for him—Merl? I imagine him pushing a cart around the library, spying on Mallory and me between the shelves.

"I had an episode, okay? I don't have *control* over it. You're not the only one."

"Forget Mallory then. What about Elaine? Or Lynette? All nice girls . . ."

"They don't matter. I'm better on my own."

Merl rattles the ice in his glass. "Do you know how many years it takes for the night sky to change? Hmm?" He takes a sip. "Thousands. But it does happen. Over centuries and centuries. A star burns out here. A new one bursts into life there. It's subtle and it takes a long long time, but eventually, one day far into the future, the sky you look up at tonight will no longer exist."

"Yeah, well. I'll be long dead before then."

"Lucky you. I hope it's a comfort. Sailors used to rely on the stars to navigate, you know. But that only works if you're traveling through space. You see, the thing is, if I go too far—like I did on this past trip—the stars aren't familiar at all." He drains his drink, smacks his lips. "Now I've answered your question. You answer mine. Mallory St. Thomas?"

"I already told you. I had a panic attack! What I want to know is: Why now? You could have knocked on my door at any other time in my life. What's so important about now?"

"Maybe I nudged you in the past, but I always hoped you'd do it on your own. This is my last resort, really." His nose is running. He wipes it with his cloak sleeve.

"Well, thanks, but no thanks. I can do just fine without your meddling."

"Look, Geoff. Your panic attacks are just an excuse. You didn't kiss Mallory St. Thomas because you were scared shitless. That's it. You're a wuss."

"I would like you to leave now. Please get out of my house."

Merl shook his head, then nodded once. "I won't bother you again." He held out his glass, and just as I went for it, he sneezed and disappeared.

The glass dropped, but this time I caught it. I stood there, a little in shock. I waited for the rush of blood to my head, even reached for the counter, but I didn't faint. I didn't.

She gave it back to me. I remember. Mallory St. Thomas. Slipped it in one of my textbooks when I wasn't looking. I found it years later. Flattened, stuck between the pages. At first I thought it was trash, a gum wrapper. When I realized what it was I kept it. Still have it. In a zip-lock baggie. Somewhere.

◇◇◇

I still sit on the porch in the evenings, watch the street, have a drink. I've allotted time specifically for this. It's a good habit. Takes my mind off things. I never look over at his hovel. Sometimes I think he's over there, sitting on his porch, watching the street, having a drink himself, not looking at my house, too. But I don't know for sure. I won't check his lawn or his mail.

I follow my routine. Do the copy. Fend off the neighbors and their "Dumble-don't!" propaganda. I have a good life. I have food and money and a porch to sit on in the evenings.

One day I pick up the phone book and smell it. Then I flip to the S's. There are twenty-five St. Thomases. I close the book. Count to a hundred. Then sharpen all my colored pencils and go back to work.

Three days later I type her name into Google. One of the results is a local newspaper website that contains her wedding announcement from sixteen years ago. To Terry H. White. That's where I'd heard the name. I must have read about it in the paper years ago.

It takes a whole week before I pick up the phone book again. There are about a million Whites. But only three Terences. I write out the addresses on a piece of paper and pin it to my bulletin board.

Later I throw it in the trash.

Then I go back, throw the phone book in after.

Only problem is one of the addresses was a street not far from where I live. And when I'm out one day I walk down, instead of past it. I've tried to forget the house number, but the only time you ever really remember something is when you try to forget it.

1136. Number on the mailbox. It's small. Yellow. Petunias in planters. SUV in the drive. The garage open, a woman wheeling her trash down to the curb. I walk faster, hoping she doesn't see me, she won't recognize me, it's not her, it's not her, it's not her.

And it's not. She's not Mallory St. Thomas. She's Mrs. Terence White.

She says good evening, and I nod and walk on.

◇◇◇

A month later there's a red FOR SALE sign in Merl's yard. The realtor has three Open Houses, but nobody's buying. The suburbanites scare away potential home-owners, warning them that the hovel is cursed. Touched by the hand of Satan, they say. No exorcism is strong enough to rid that place of its demons.

W.A.R.T. starts a petition to have the neighborhood committee purchase the property and tear down the place, use the land to start a community garden or build a clubhouse or pool or something. Everyone signs. They skip my house when they're going door-to-door, but I go out to them on the street with a ballpoint pen, take the clipboard, and ask: what line?

It's about time I started making friends around here.

◇◇◇

Bulldozers are brought in and we form a huddle on the sidewalk out front, holding champagne glasses. We chit-chat. We say good riddance. About time. We watch the hovel collapse in on itself like a tiered cake. The crowd gives a little cheer. A sigh of relief escapes from many who feared that some charm might have made the place indestructible. We pop the cork and clink glasses. Gwen Pendrake sprinkles bubbly on Lance Dulack's leaves.

Across the street, there's a boy sitting in a tree. He's been watching the whole thing. But when I rush over and take a look the branches are empty. A woman comes out of the house in a yellow bathrobe and asks what I'm doing on her lawn. It's Vivienne LeFeigh.

"Have you seen him?" I say.

"Do I know you?" she says, squinting.

"Sorry," I tell her. "Wrong house."

I return to my side of the street. Most of the drama is over. The sidewalk in front of his hovel clearing. Everyone goes back to their kids and crock-pots and the evening news. Marty Pendrake trails behind his wife and her urn.

Soon there's nothing left but an ugly pit in the ground.

◇◇◇

I can't sleep anymore. The bed's cold. Why have I never realized how cold the bed is?

Nothing helps. Books. Shoes. Pennies. Pencils. I sit on the porch and stare at the streetlights.

One night I can't take it anymore. I go out to the porch, but I can't sit still. I look over at his yard. I pace. I walk down the porch stairs, across my lawn, and over to the pit.

It's not very big, not very deep. Pretty unimpressive. About the size of a backyard swimming pool. I squint at the dark down below.

It occurred to me the other day that if Merl's seen my past he's probably seen my future. He must have always known I would betray him. If he were here now I'd ask him what Future Me is like. But maybe I already know. I hope not.

I might even ask him to deliver a letter: *Dear Future Me* . . .

But then what? I don't know what to write next: *I hope you're happy? Take care?*

Moonlight falling. A baby cries. Naked, on a mound of dirt, there in the middle of the pit. I climb down and take him into my arms. Younger than I've ever seen him. He's colicky. A newborn. His eyes an empty blue. He hasn't seen anything yet. He knows nothing. I rub his back. Whisper shhh, it's okay, shhh. I hold him up to the stars and say, see? Look. See? He falls asleep against my chest. I feel the barely-there weight of him. I watch his face scrunch, his nose twitch, like before a sneeze. His tiny mouth opens and closes in a yawn.

I stay in this moment, knowing it can't last, that time is mobile, time is swift, soon it will leave me here, holding nothing but my own arms.

Journal of a Cyclops

I was born with one eye. The doctor and nurses on duty at St. Alice's maternity ward on the day of my delivery (June 6, 2004) were ready and waiting for my arrival, equipped with their APGAR test, which stands for: Appearance Pulse Grimace Activity Respiration and is a rating of 1–10 for "newborn viability." (I'm copying this out of my anatomy and physiology textbook—*Understanding the Human Body*, page 113—after looking up *birth defects* in the index, although Mother doesn't like that word. "It's a birth *gift*, Owen." But what the gift part of it is I'll never know.) I picture the hospital staff standing in their blue scrubs, all in a row, with clipboards and calculators and maybe a white board to work out the mathematical equation of my future survivability. Despite my deformity (a word Mother hates even worse), I scored a six.

My parents were like any new parents; when Mother was pregnant and they were asked whether they wanted a boy or a girl, they gave the typical reply: we just want a healthy baby with all his (or her) fingers and toes. Too bad for me, they forgot to include eyes on that wish list. If I had it my way I'd have come out with an extra digit or two, or missing a thumb. Maybe if they'd been more specific in their prayers for my normality, I might have come out different (metaphorical prayers, of course, not religious ones, since Mother and Father, and I guess that includes me too, are atheists, which means we don't believe in God or asking him for favors like babies with the normal number of eyes.)

The doctor and nurses counted only one: a single blue marble, roaming from startled face to startled face, smack dab in the middle of my forehead, blinking (which, technically, if you think about it, is a *wink*) back at them.

Hello.

"How about those fingers?" Father said, only half joking, at Mother's side. They were both spent from the labor, a nervousness growing between them at the silence that pervaded the delivery room while the hospital staff stared, transfixed by the All-Important Eye (AIE).

One of the nurses was sick and stumbled out the door, down the hall to the bathroom.

"Never seen anything like it," said another with a stronger stomach.

"Take it to the NICU," the doctor whispered.

"Where are they taking him?" Mother asked. "I want to hold him. Don't I get to hold him?"

"In good time," the doctor said.

Tests were performed. Father gave full permission: X-rays, MRIs, DNA mapping. Experts were called in. They marveled. Could I see out of that thing? What about neural function? Brain wiring? After three days of intensive medical examination it was determined that despite the unusual number of orbital sockets the AIE was perfectly normal. I had decreased peripheral vision, but the abnormality was not harmful to my overall health and well-being.

Did you get that, Dr. Moher? "Not harmful to my overall health and well-being."

The medical term for my condition is *synophthalmia*, which means that the bone and skin tissue that should have grown between my two orbital cavities in-utero, did not. Over 99 percent of fetuses with synophthalmia are miscarried and of the 1 percent that come to term, I have been the only known synophthalmiac that has been viable for longer than a week. The doctors predicted I wouldn't make it to my first birthday. I am now thirteen years old.

But I guess you know that from my medical file. I'm writing it in here, because when you gave me this notebook you said to start at the beginning and tell it like a story.

I have my own copy of the file. (Okay, I hacked Dr. Zabinski's computer. You can't tell Mother because of doctor-patient confidentiality.) I don't know if Dr. Z gave you the manuscript of his book (*Cyclopia: An Ophthalmological Case Study*), but if you do have it you'll see the photos. Thirteen of them—one for every year. If you stack them together you can make a flipbook. You can see me grow up like time-lapse photography. Like a flower blooming or a piece of fruit decaying in seconds.

There I am, a little one-AIEd baby lying in an incubator, a speck of a person, maybe I'm even cute (in a freakish way). Watch and I'll start expanding, losing baby fat, clambering awkwardly to my feet, growing taller and rounder, hair filling in, holes gaping from lost teeth; braces appear, a monocle too; blackheads burst to life; until, finally, you see me today: Owen James Pollup, obese, cyclopic, home-schooled, single-child teen that I am.

You probably think that I feel sorry for myself, but I don't. I'm writing this for one purpose only: so you'll convince Mother to let me go to public school once summer's over. She says she trusts you, Dr. Moher; she'll agree if you say yes (she's sure you won't). She thinks she's protecting me—high school can be cruel, I get that—but don't I at least deserve the chance?

◇◇◇

Every morning this is my schedule: I wake up and rub sleep crust from my AIE. I use the toilet, brush my teeth, shower, then come down for breakfast. While Mother makes pancakes or oatmeal or omelets with goat cheese (my favorite) I sit at the counter and we review. Sometimes it's Algebra formulas (X-equals-negative-B-plus-or-minus-radical-B-squared-minus-four-A-C-all-over-two-A), others U.S. presidents (Wash, Ad, Jeff, Mad, Mon, Ad, Jack) or historical dates (the War of 1812). A week ago it was Biology vocab (I'm always mixing up meiosis and mitosis). Father reads the paper in his blue button-down with the Red Lobster nametag.

Our air-conditioning broke the night before, and even with all the fans on and the windows open, there was barely a breeze in the kitchen. Sweat dripped down my forehead, high-diving off my nose and onto the drawings of cells dividing on my workbook page.

Some of it got in my AIE. I took off my monocle and rubbed at it.

"Are you hurting?" Mother asked.

"Just sweaty."

Sometimes I get these headaches. Chronic migraines, Mother tells Dr. Zabinski. It's an exaggeration. They really aren't that bad and they don't occur more than a few times a month. If I stay out of the light or lie down with my AIE closed it goes away.

"Hades in here." Father peeled the wet shirt off his back. "Guy said he'd be here noon at the latest."

Mother fanned herself with a placemat. Her left eye is a hair higher than the right, which makes her look slightly puzzled even when she's not.

"Maybe you should go lie down." She put a hand on my cheek. "I'll bring you a glass of water and your drops."

"I'm fine." I swatted her away. "I just got to get out of this house."

"Good idea. How about Father sets up the sprinkler in the backyard? I'll make us a pitcher of lemonade."

"Actually, I was thinking, maybe I could go to the pool," I said.

Mother's brow contorted into a predictable half-sympathetic, half-skeptical frown. I turned to Father. His eyes are brown and close together, with a squinty quality, like he's perpetually looking into the sun. He raised his paper to cover them.

"Owen." Mother used that stupid delicate tone she always uses to let me down. ("Owen, I'm sorry but you can't go to the comic book store . . . Owen, you know city park is off-limits . . . Owen, contacts are just too risky . . .").

"I promise I'll be careful. I won't look anyone in the eye."

"Owen, you don't even know how to swim," she said (as if that were the issue).

"I can stand in the shallow end. Or I'll just sit on the edge. I don't care."

"What if you get chlorine in your eye? We don't know how it would react. Is going to the pool worth being blinded over?"

"That's not why you won't let me go and you know it."

Mother sighed. "Mitch," she said to Father. "Please."

"I don't know," Father said. "Maybe he has a point? It's awful hot and he's all cooped up—"

"But the sprinkler," she said. I could see it in her face. Memories of childhood Owen running around with yellow float-ies on his arms.

"You can't keep me in the backyard forever," I said. "I'm not your pet."

"Oh, Owen," she said, tears standing in her eyes. Mother can cry in an instant. She uses it to her advantage.

"Don't worry," I said. "I'll just hide in my room. I hate to be such an *eyesore*." I knocked the stool over on my way out.

◇◇◇

When you're thirteen and not allowed to leave the house except for optometrist, ophthalmologist, and child psychologist (thanks, Dr. Moher) appointments, you develop hobbies fast. So here's what my room looks like when you walk in:

The first thing you'll notice is the desk with the computer console. Two PCs, one laptop, and three dinosaurs I rescued from the grave. Next to this is my worktable where there's a soldering station, a magnifying lens, and the circuit board I've been working on. Across from this, by the window, is my telescope and star maps from my Astronomy phase two years ago. On the shelf over my bed are about twenty cardboard boxes of puzzles. The two bookshelves Father and I built together are filled with *Star Wars*, *Dune*, and other sci-fi/fantasy series. Above those is a big bulletin board with photos—a black silhouette of Mother, Father holding a lobster claw, a self-portrait in a mirror with the camera lens blocking my AIE. I turned my closet into a dark room a year ago. I went digital later, mucked around in Photoshop, but even that got old.

I took off my monocle, put on my safety goggles, and sat down at my circuit board, sorting through a box of microchips. A minute later Mother knocked on my door. I ignored it. I was sick of her slanted face.

"Hey O." Father. He rarely came to my room. "Can I come in?"

I asked for a lock on my door like a million times, but Mother says too much privacy can be dangerous: "What if something happens and we can't get to you? What then?"

Father was on my side that time. "There are just some things teenage boys feel more comfortable doing behind locked doors."

"Yeah," I agreed. A look passed between them. "Wait. What?"

Of course Mother got her way. They gave me a *Do Not Disturb* sign to hang on my doorknob as if our house were a hotel. They promised to always knock.

"I don't want to talk to you." I bent lower over the magnifying glass.

"Okay." He didn't leave. I could hear his weight shifting out in the hall. "Hey O."

"You're going to be late," I said.

"Remember what I always told you when you were a kid? Remember what I said?"

I imagined him standing on the other side in his lame Red Lobster dress slacks, tartar sauce stains down the side.

"Yeah," I said. It's embarrassing. He can be so cheesy sometimes. "Beauty is in the eye of the beholder." I rolled my AIE. "So what? Big deal."

"That's right." Then he added the part he always did: "Eye," he said and I could almost see his squinty smile through the door. "Singular."

◇◇◇

The AC man came at three. The doorbell rang and Mother answered it. I was half tempted to spy. When I was younger I used to sit at the top of the stairs and peer down through the rungs at Girl Scouts, door-to-door salesmen, neighbors on our front stoop (they were rarely invited in).

That seems silly now. It's not like I don't have cable. Or the internet.

So I went back to my work, testing used hard drives, connecting wires. I was super-gluing a missing J key onto a keyboard when I heard someone on the stairs.

"Go away, Mother. I'm working."

The footsteps stopped. I crossed the room, bent down, and looked under the door. Two feet appeared in the crack: Converse shoes colored with Sharpie.

I stumbled to my feet, across the room, and into my closet.

For almost a full minute nothing happened. I left the closet door ajar and waited, watching the empty room. Then the knob turned, the door opened, and a boy slipped inside.

He was wearing black jeans (beltless, too big around the waist) and a red T-shirt. At first he just stood in the center of my room, turning a complete circle to take everything in. Then he began to snoop. He walked over to the telescope and peeked inside. He looked at my photos and books, trailing his finger along the spines. He touched the tools I had sitting out on my worktable, the mini-screwdriver, the soldering laser. A vent rattled, making me jump. I knocked over a tin of photo developer. Cool air blew through the baseboard.

He walked over to the closet and my breath caught. I backed away slowly, pressing all the way against the wall, getting tangled in the clothesline I used to clip photos. His eyes were wide, black. Like the way the AIE must look after Dr. Z puts in the stingy drops so my pupil dilates and he can see inside with his little light, probably to the back of my head.

I clamped my hands over the AIE. I watched him through the space in my fingers. Leave, I thought. Please just leave. But beneath that hope was another and this one moved me forward, not back. My hands left my forehead, they brushed the back of the closet door and the crack widened.

"I . . . see . . . you," I whispered.

The boy screamed and tripped over himself.

He lay sprawled on the floor. I opened the door and his two eyes found my one.

"Hi." I offered my hand. "I'm Owen."

But he scrambled from the room, thundered through the hall, down the stairs, and out the front door.

I went to the window and watched him meet his father at the curb. The AC man was yelling. He collared the boy into his truck and they drove away.

I waved furiously, but neither looked up.

◇◇◇

He was back three days later, out on the front stoop, trying to see past the curtains in the entry windows, ringing the bell over and over. Mother was at the grocery, Father at work.

("What do you do if someone comes to the house when we aren't home?" Mother asked in one of our "Pollup Family Safety Training Sessions."

"I stay in my room," I said.

"You stay in your room.")

The bell was still ringing. I watched him from my window. He was wearing a digital camera around his neck like a tourist. He must have rung for a good ten minutes, before I went down and cracked the door, just enough so he could hear (but not see) me.

"Go away," I said. "My parents aren't here."

"I know." He pressed his face in to get a glimpse. I slammed the door shut.

"Sorry," he called from the other side. "You don't have to let me in. I just—it's—you have a really cool room."

"Um, thanks." I opened the door far enough so he could see me. He didn't flinch or anything, which was a good sign.

"Sorry I snooped. My dad was real mad when he found out."

"I don't care."

"Did you build all those computers?"

"Most of the desktops. Not the Macbook. I'm working on a 96 model now. It's more complicated than the 92."

"Can I see it? I'm Darien by the way." He thrust his hand through the gap.

I know what you're thinking, Dr. Moher: I should have known better. But I had this vision of Darien playing videogames with me, sharing a bowl of popcorn or Doritos. And even as I was leading him upstairs, wondering if this boy might be my future best friend (if such a thing were possible) and my AIE was throbbing like it does before a headache (throbbing with portent?)

some part of me was saying: what are you doing, he's already seen your stuff, Mother will kill you if she finds out, he's faking, he doesn't care about you, why does he have that camera?

"Woah." He started picking up random things—an old Nintendo controller, a glass paperweight, a piece of meteor rock—going "Look at this!" and "No way!" and "Kick ass!"

"It's all right, I guess," I said, pretending not to be flattered.

"How come I've never seen you around?" Darien asked.

"I'm homeschooled."

"Is it because of your . . ." He put a finger to his forehead. "You know."

That made me self-conscious, so I took off my monocle and put on the tinted sun-goggles. "Mother says kids can be mean."

"That's bogus. Lots of kids get picked on. You think I don't get picked on? You think I have tons of friends?"

"Maybe. I don't know."

"Well, I don't. I'm not popular." The way he said it—*popular*—it was like, maybe he could be?

"Why do you have that camera?" I asked.

"School project."

"But it's summer."

"Yeah, I know. Summer school. It's like extra classes you take in the summer to get ahead. You wouldn't know about it."

"What are you studying?"

"You want to play Super Smash Bros?" He held up the game.

Did I ever. But still. I hesitated. "I don't know. Mother will be back soon."

"Why do you call her that?"

"What?"

"Never mind. Just one game?"

So we played. And: It. Was. Awesome. I'd only ever played one-player before and it's nothing like having two. Darien was good, but he wasn't *really* good like I was. It was easy when you put in the hours I did. I let him win a few rounds. I think he could tell.

"No handicaps," he said. "I want to win fair and square."

We were on the fifth or sixth game when a car door slammed in the driveway. Any second and Mother would ask me to help with the groceries.

I clicked off the TV. "You have to go."

"Do you mind if I take a pic first?"

I thought he meant of the room. Like maybe he wanted to do his the same? I told him, yeah sure, whatever. But then his hands were prying the sun-goggles off my face and the camera was flashing right in my AIE. I was blinded—all I could see was a yellow starburst.

"I'll go out the back," he said. "Play again soon?"

"Uh, yeah." I rubbed flecks of red, gold, and green from my AIE. Slowly the colors cleared and I could see my room again.

◇◇◇

That night we had dinner at Red Lobster. I wore my sun-goggles, trying not to think about how Darien's hands felt, ripping them off my AIE, snapping that photo.

"Owen," Mother said. "You've barely touched your crab legs."

"Would you like something else?" Father said. "Some jumbo shrimp?" He gets our meals complimentary, which is why my diet consists primarily of seafood.

"I'm not hungry."

"Is this about the pool thing?" Mother said. "Because I called the YMCA and one of the lifeguards said he'd open their pool an hour early for you. That way you could go in the morning and swim on your own."

"How's that sound?" Father asked.

"I don't care about the pool anymore. I want to go to school in the fall."

The waitress brought the shrimp Father ordered. She set it next to me, avoiding AIE contact. I think Father's told his staff I have permanent pink eye or something.

"I know you don't think I can handle it, but I'm ready," I said.

"What does Dr. Moher say?" Mother asked.

"He says it's an . . . option." (Okay, I lied. When I brought it up at our last session and you said I should take things one step at a time? I shouldn't risk doing anything too damaging to my already fragile psyche? What am I supposed to do with that?)

"Hmm, does he?" Mother said.

"He says I'm missing out on peer bonding. That my socialization skills have stagnated."

"That sounds a lot like your *Psychology, Syndrome, and Society* textbook," Mother said.

"Whatever."

"You should really try one of these shrimp, O," Father said, cocktail sauce on his chin.

"Owen, honey," Mother said. "I know you want to be like those other kids, but the truth is you're not. And it's not because of your birth gift. It's because of your intelligence and your kindness and your charm. The fact of the matter is that you're simply too good for public school."

"You're saying it has nothing to do with this?" I pointed at my AIE.

"Of course not," Mother said. "Is it part of you? Yes. But is it who you are? No. Never."

"So then you won't mind if I just—" and I took the goggles off.

Several things happened in quick succession: 1.) The waitress, who was refilling Father's water glass, saw my AIE and was struck dumb—she just kept pouring and pouring until ice and water overflowed into his lap. 2.) Father, who was reaching over to steal the hushpuppies off my plate, yelped at the sudden burst of cold in his crotch. 3.) Every Thursday night patron of Red Lobster looked over at the sound of said yelp and followed the gaze of the young waitress to the culprit of this disturbance: the offending AIE. 4.) Mother clamped hold of my wrist and dragged me out to the parking lot. And finally: 5.) I threw the sun-goggles at her feet.

"What is *wrong* with you?" she said. We faced off, three feet from our car.

"Why don't we play a game, Mother?" I was fighting back tears. They always stung, sometimes they brought on the migraines. "See if we can figure it out. I spy with my little AIE . . ."

It was a game we used to play when I was a kid. Dr. Zabinski taught it to my parents to test the muscular movement in my AIE. It was a peripheral vision test. They would move an object around the room and tell me I could only look for it with my AIE ("I spy apple. I spy pencil"). I wasn't allowed to move my head. Sometimes it hurt to play.

"With my little AIE, what do I spy?"

"Quit it, Owen. Get in the car." She was crying a little, just barely.

I was laughing. I was hysterical. I was thinking about all those people in Red Lobster (how many millions of times had we had family dinner there?), how they had only ever really seen me tonight. It was hilarious! It was hilarious!

"Owen, please. It's not funny."

Oh, but it was. I was doubled over. I put a hand on the car to steady myself. In the side mirror, I looked at myself. "I spy AIE." It was so funny it hurt. "There AIE am."

◇◇◇

The photo looked fake: face blurred, AIE out of focus. Like I could have two of them. Like they had merged because the camera moved.

Darien didn't ask for another.

We were sitting together at the foot of my bed, playing Mario Kart. When I brought up the picture he paused the game, pulled the camera out of his pocket, and showed me.

"You've got to delete it," I said. "You didn't . . . show anyone?"

Darien shrugged, pocketing the camera. "It barely even looks like you."

"I know, but . . ."

"But what?" He picked up the controller.

"I don't know."

"Okay then. Let's play."

This time I forgot to lose. Or maybe I just didn't want to. (Which do you think, Dr. Moher? My subconscious acting up?) I beat him six times in a row; it wasn't even close.

"God damn it!" He flung the controller against the wall. Batteries clattered out the back. "Fuck it. You suck. It's not fair."

"We can put on the handicap," I offered lamely.

"You're only good because you play all the time. Because you don't have a life outside this stupid room."

He was right. It wasn't talent. Just practice. I felt my AIE pounding.

"Look." Darien went to get the controller. "I'm sorry, okay? Please don't cry."

"I'm not." Really, I wasn't.

"You want to go again?"

"It's not my fault," I said. "I want to leave more than anything."

"What's stopping you? Your parents? So what? Sneak out."

"You mean like . . . by myself?"

"Why not? Run away if you can't stand it so bad."

It had never occurred to me before. It wasn't like there were bars on my window.

"If you could get out, where would you go?" Darien asked.

"I don't know. The pool, maybe?"

"You've never been swimming?" Darien laughed. "It's nothing special. But I can take you."

"What about—well, you know . . ."

"Your eye? Who cares? You can wear goggles. Nobody will see."

"But Mother—"

"Mother Shmother." Darien picked up his backpack. "Tomorrow? You'll sneak out?"

"I'll sneak out?" I said and Darien clapped a hand on my shoulder. "Yeah, I'll sneak out."

◇◇◇

Aquamarine—the color of pool water. But in my sun-goggles it was brown. The chlorine, I could smell. It had a sharp chemical scent that made me dizzy. The sun was high overhead, sweat pooling in my sandals. Darien led me through the metal gate leading out to the pool deck. He waved at a huddle of teenagers tanning and playing cards. They visored their hands over their eyes, registering only mild interest when they saw me, his tag along.

Darien set down the cooler, stocked with soda and turkey sandwiches, between two lounge chairs. He threw down his beach towel and stripped off his shirt. He looked tan, but that could have just been the goggles. I tried not to think about the doughy chest beneath my own shirt. I sat down on one of the chairs and took off my sandals. A few of the kids were still watching.

"Do you know them?" I asked. "They keep looking over here."

"Just ignore them. Let's go off the diving board. I'll teach you to cannonball."

"Go ahead. I'll just sit for a while."

"Come on. We're here to swim."

"I don't feel like it."

Darien threw up his hands. I watched him wait in line, then go off the board. He bounced twice, each time gaining height, then his body made a clean arc up and out into the air. It was a smooth dive—graceful—not a cannonball. He surfaced and called out to me, flinging water with his hand. It left splotches on the concrete. He climbed out on the ladder, trunks dripping wet.

"You're missing out," he said.

That's when the teenagers walked over, the five of them. They smelled like coconut oil. There was an awkward pause and then a chorus of heys passed through the group.

"This is Owen." Darien's brow raised and all eyes shifted to me.

"What's with the goggles?" one guy said. "You know they're for *in* the pool, right?"

A few snickered. Darien laughed along. They were all looking at my forehead, trying to see beyond the tinted lens.

"The sun's too bright," I said. "I have a headache."

"Maybe that's because they're too tight on your head."

"Yeah, you should loosen them."

"Take them off, give your eye a rest."

"I'm getting in the pool now." I got up and padded down to the shallow end.

"His shirt's still on," someone said behind me, adding to the laughter.

I sat on the edge and dipped my feet in. I half-expected Darien to follow. He didn't. He looked happy, but he clearly didn't fit in with the others, who were all taller, broader, blonder. I watched one of them gesturing, like he was removing a pair of invisible glasses.

(You saw this coming, didn't you, Dr. Moher? You're not surprised. Silly Owen. What a dupe. Thought Darien actually wanted to be his friend. But don't you see? If I can survive this, I can survive anything.)

Darien came over and sat down beside me.

"I want to go home," I said.

"We just got here. You haven't even been in the water yet."

He swirled his foot, making a little whirlpool. I scooted away. He splashed me. I splashed back. He stood up and cannonballed in. The water he displaced soaked my shirt. He came up laughing, like it was all in good fun.

"Stop," I said.

"You're such a party pooper." He ran his fingers through his wet hair. He waded back over to the edge and climbed out.

"Why do you like them?" I said.

"I don't know. They're cool."

"They're jerks. Why don't we go back and play Mario?"

"Why? So you can beat me again?"

"No."

"One cannonball," he said.

I didn't want to.

"Maybe with a really big splash you'll even get a few of them wet."

I really didn't want to.

"Come on. It's easy. I'll show you." He stood up, held out his hand. I took it.

We stood in line together, eyes darting at us like flies. I took my shirt off, but left the goggles on. Darien said he'd go first. "Tuck your knees in and hold them really tight against your chest. Try to hit on your butt and lower back for the best splash effect." He climbed the three-step ladder.

I watched his technique. Again, the two bounces. At the pinnacle of the second, he tucked in and executed a perfect front flip before cannonballing into the water.

"Show off," I muttered.

"Don't worry about the flip part," Darien called.

The diving board was rough beneath my feet. I gripped the metal safety bars, hesitant to let go where they stopped. Two more steps to the end of the board. I took one, close enough. I bent my legs in a test bounce, and the board sprang beneath me.

"You can do it," Darien said, treading water below. The lifeguard blew the whistle at him, motioning for him to swim over to the ladder.

Two bounces and a leap. Two bounces and a leap. I took my first bounce and accidentally hit the board at an angle. It flung me forward—out, not up. I left the board too soon, there wasn't time to tuck anything, I was out in open air, face planting, belly flopping, *smack!*

Water rushed up my nose, bubbles flew up all around me in a net. I tried to kick up, but I was sinking. I had my AIE squeezed tight and when I opened it to get my bearings all I could see was a haze of blue. A darker blue, a deeper blue—not aquamarine like I thought—colder. And it was burning me, it was right inside my AIE.

My goggles, I realized.

And there they were, floating above me like a murky strand of seaweed. I lunged for them, I reached, but they were caught. I yanked and they yanked back.

It was Darien, floating above me, he was pulling on them, he wanted to help me, he was going to save me? He wouldn't let me drown. But he was kicking down, his feet shoving hard against my chest, and we were struggling underwater and I couldn't—I couldn't—

He breast-stroked up to the surface, the goggles clutched in his hand. The surface, where eyes blinked, distortions in the water, faces looking down at me, all of them watching, waiting for me to come up, so they could know me for what I really am.

Lipless

The invitation came in the mail and his wife saw the name before he did and she said, I didn't know Devin was getting married, and that's when he knew—not in the gym that one time, or on their road trip to Boston, not at the wrestling match or even during the ice storm—no, that was the moment, Dev's name on his wife's lips, Marcus knew for sure that he was in love with his college roommate and would never tell him. They were standing in the kitchen and his wife had torn into the fancy envelope—this struck him as rude, it being from Devin, although it had been addressed to both of them, of course, and she had every right to open it. He didn't like how illogically possessive he felt of Devin and he didn't want Kara to notice, so he stuck his head back in the fridge. Rummaged around. The beer already in his hand.

He came out with a bowl of guacamole. He didn't like guac. Kara was examining their calendar. He put it back.

"Crap," she said. "We have Newlywed the same weekend."

Marcus wasn't sure which trumped the other: his disappointment or relief. Of all the ways in which he'd imagined seeing Devin again, none of them had involved a church or a bride or an audience of strangers in pews.

"I'll call Liam," Kara said. "I'm sure we can re-schedule."

Her purse was on the counter. She went for her cell.

"Don't bother," Marcus said, trying to sound indifferent.

"Are you sure?"

"The study's more important."

This was the wrong excuse. Since they began the Newlywed Study at the Florida university where Kara worked, Marcus had found it incredibly dull. He'd been trying to convince her they should drop it since the first session and routinely complained about it every six months when the next one rolled around. They'd signed up less for the money—it only paid a hundred dollars per session, which often took up to four hours, and the surveys that had to be filled out before and after took another three—and more as a favor for Liam, a colleague of Kara's and the lead on the project. Fewer couples had signed up in response to the online ads than he'd expected.

"Oh, so now you're into the study?" she said.

"I just don't like weddings, is all," Marcus said.

Kara frowned. She knew her husband better than that. Marcus *did* hate weddings—at least the ceremony part—but he loved receptions. He was a terrible dancer, but that was kind of the point. You weren't supposed to dance well at weddings. They were safe places where middle-aged uncles and great aunts did the electric slide, where the flower girl and ring bearer danced the funky chicken, where the Macarena made a sickeningly nostalgic comeback, and anyone under the age of thirty—Marcus and Kara were included in that group, but just barely—felt less pressure to look good while dancing.

Their favorite dates had been to weddings—of cousins, neighbors, friends. Kara had never seen Marcus dance anywhere else like he danced at weddings. They tried clubs, but with music too loud to talk over and crowds of twentysomethings all trying to look sexy, they really weren't their scene. She'd even signed them up for dancing lessons, but it was the wrong move. He was too self-conscious at them—the point of dancing lessons is not to dance *badly*, but to get better—and it felt more like labor than play so they stopped going. Wedding receptions remained the only place Marcus could dance like the skinny white man he was and not care what anyone else thought.

"What's going on with you?" Kara said.

"Nothing." He tried to open his beer and the cap about shredded his hand.

"Those aren't twist-offs," she said.

"Obviously." He sucked at the ridges cut into his palm and glared at her as if she'd purposely bought this brand of beer so this would happen.

Kara opened a drawer and handed him a bottle opener. Something about the way she did that—heaved open the shitty silverware drawer that always stuck, held out the opener to him, handle out, the sharp part tucked into her palm, shoved the drawer closed with her hip, all in one startlingly fluid motion— made him feel so immensely his love for this woman, he knew he couldn't stand to be in the same room as Devin and her. It might kill him. His heart would literally explode.

"What?" Kara said.

He could feel himself gawking.

"If you don't want to go to this wedding, just say so. He's *your* friend."

"I don't want to go," he said.

"Fine," she said. "His fiancée has terrible taste anyway. I mean, look at this."

She held up the invitation. She was talking about the image of a dove inside a heart plastered to the corner, complete with craft feathers and glitter, but Marcus's eye landed on the name of the bride-to-be.

"Rachel Kennedy!" he said.

"Oh, you know her?"

"Barely." He popped the cap off his beer and took a swig.

He sensed Kara had more to say about the invitation, perhaps the melodramatic religious phrasing (Marcus remembered Devin was Catholic)—*Please join us in celebration when, together with their Lord, Rachel and Devin form a union in holy matrimony and the two become one*—or the curlicued font, but she hesitated to say it now that she knew Marcus knew Rachel. She must have felt some gravity in this knowledge and so, instead, she attached the invitation to the fridge with a magnet in the shape of an owl. She stuck this next to the gaudy, bejeweled dove as if to apologize for her earlier mockery. The two birds stared at Marcus with an unwelcome, feathered camaraderie.

"In case you change your mind."

◇◇◇

In the week leading up to their first Newlywed session (this was nearly three years ago, two months into their marriage), Marcus couldn't help thinking of it as a sex study.

A brief unit in an introductory Psych course in college had instilled in him a certain appetite for that kind of thing and in one semester, to the neglect of the reading assigned in his actual major (English Literature), he'd devoured the Kinsey reports, the Masters and Johnson research, and the findings of any recent sex studies he could get his hands on. Something about the scientific pursuit of the most primal form of human desire drew him in. Either that, or he was just a horny teenager not getting any at the time.

What *else* would you ask recently married couples about? Their finances? Probably. Their communication skills? Definitely. What they argued about, how they made up. He knew these were the more reasonable concerns the Newlywed Study would most likely address, but whenever he thought about it in the days leading up to their first session an image sprang to mind of he and Kara fucking on a table—why a table? something about cop-drama interrogation sequences was mixed up in here—with electrodes taped to their temples, chests, and wrists, wires ensnaring their bodies as they moved and machines spat out readings and scientists in white lab coats took notes behind a one-way mirror, impressed by both his form and stamina.

Only in his head was what he and Kara did called "fucking." This word expressed a violence that did not translate to their actual bedroom. In their married life, they did not "fuck." And it was nothing so mawkish as "love-making." It was "having sex." Or maybe "sharing sex." Yes, he thought. That was good. He'd have to remember that for the interview. The distinction seemed important. He heard himself stopping himself midsentence—"no," he'd say, "it's not *having* so much as *sharing*."

The night before the interview they each had to fill out a survey about the current state of their marriage. There were sex questions on there, but they were mostly about frequency. Marcus put down three times a week and told himself he wasn't exaggerating, or, at least, not by much. The instructions were to fill out the surveys separately—which they did, Marcus at the kitchen table, Kara at her desk—and to *not* share their answers with their partner—which they ignored and promptly did anyway.

"Three times a week," Kara scoffed.

"So? What did you put?" Marcus scanned down her list of answers to number 56. "Point five? Point five! What does that even mean? How can you have half a sex?"

"The question posed it weekly. And it's been about once every other week so . . ."

"Every other week!" Marcus said.

Later, this became a joke between them, through the short-hand couples often have. Marcus would start something and Kara would shrug him off, claiming to be too tired or gassy or not in the mood, and he'd screw up his face in the imitation of a boy denied a cookie. "Not even half?" he'd say and they'd laugh until their sides split.

"I'm just being honest," Kara said, about the survey. "I can change it to once a week, if you want."

Marcus shook his head. He trusted her calculation more than his own.

"How could we have fallen so far behind our quota!" he said. "Quick! To the bedroom!"

He was being facetious, of course, but part of him was actually concerned. There was the old coin-jar joke about the first year of marriage, but maybe that only applied to the first year of the relationship? Kara and he had dated for two years in Ohio and been engaged for one. Had their sex life really leveled off already?

He threw the survey down and scooped Kara out of her chair. Well, his intention was to scoop, but Marcus wasn't exactly in shape and Kara wasn't the daintiest of wives, so this masculine show of romance proved to be more of an awkward maneuver— his arms crunched by the backs of her knees, a near elbow to the eye, then, finally, the old heave-ho.

He took two steps with her in his arms and collapsed. Kara checked to see if he was hurt through her laughter.

"Who needs a bed?" she said, kissing him.

He'd never loved her more.

◇◇◇

After that, the Newlywed session itself proved to be anticlimactic.

The interview was held in a spare room at the university labeled "lounge," but it was about the size of a large walk-in closet and smelled vaguely of urine. Its only furnishings included a small maroon sofa and a coffee table. There wasn't a one-way mirror or even an interviewer, per se, just a proctor and what looked to be a security camera in the corner near the ceiling. They were each handed a series of manila envelopes, numbered one to ten, containing "scenarios" that they were supposed to talk through together at their leisure. Then they were left alone.

Marcus tried to read Kara's reaction to this experimental design. She was, after all, a sociologist herself, although her research on group hysteria had nothing to do with Liam's on married couples. If she was unimpressed (as Marcus was), she didn't show it.

His first card, extracted from its envelope, read: YOUR SPOUSE WANTS TO HAVE A CHILD, BUT YOU'RE NOT READY. HOW DO YOU DEAL WITH THIS?

"What's yours say?" he asked. Kara hesitated. She glanced at the camera before handing him her card.

Predictably, the inverse: YOU WANT TO HAVE A CHILD, BUT YOUR SPOUSE IS NOT READY. HOW DO YOU DEAL WITH THIS?

Their eyes met and he had to look away to keep from laughing. Surely, she wasn't taking this seriously.

They'd been told to act natural, to speak to each other as they would privately in their home, but clearly this was impossible. As they gave their answers, perched on opposite ends of the couch, addressing the camera more than each other, it became increasingly apparent to Marcus that this study was not meant for them. The questions were designed to locate a couple's weak spot, but Kara and he were so in sync that these hypothetical conflicts were bogus. They spent the next several hours performing what felt like soliloquies from a marital self-help book:

"I would communicate my concerns, but give him enough time to know his own mind better, so we could make a rational decision together."

"We would sit down and review the credit card statements, then come up with a household budget we could agree upon."

"Don't worry," Devin said. "I'll spot you."

The metal grips on the bar cut into his palms. When Devin lifted it from the racks, Marcus's arms dropped beneath the weight, the bar thunking into his chest.

"Ow," Marcus said. "That's gonna bruise."

Devin laughed. "Sorry. I should have helped lower it. Okay, now press it overhead."

Marcus tried. He did. He could feel the blood rushing to his face as he strained. He got it up over his chest for a second and immediately dropped it back.

"Try not to let it all the way down. The point is to keep it suspended at all times. Come on. Let's see if we can do ten of them."

Marcus couldn't make it past six. Each time he dropped it. His chest felt more than a little bruised.

"Maybe we should try some with just the bar," Devin said. He lifted it back into the rack, then removed the weights.

The bar alone was better. Marcus made it successfully through ten reps, only dropping it on his chest the last three times. He sat up and Devin handed him a water bottle.

"Well done. I'll show you the pull-up bars next."

It was a weird experience. Marcus hated every bit of the exercise—the dumbbell curls, the medicine ball, squats, sit-ups, all of it—it was painful and exhausting and made him nauseous and why the hell would anyone *enjoy* putting their body through this? But every so often Devin would pat him on the back or speak an encouraging word or say something nice like—"Oh man, the ladies will be lining up at our door"—and Marcus's heart would pound a little harder, and he'd push himself a little further.

They ended with a cool-down on the treadmills. By the end, Marcus was feeling light-headed. He'd been burping up last night's lasagna dinner and when they returned to the locker rooms, he knew more was coming up.

Devin, who hadn't noticed Marcus was feeling ill, was talking about breakfast. "What you've got to eat after a work-out like that is a big ole omelet. Egg whites only. Trust me. That's the best protein."

Marcus ducked into a stall and vomited mostly water. He slipped down to the cold blue floor, a muscle twitching in his back.

"Hey," Devin called. "You okay?"

Marcus thought he was going to pass out, but then didn't. He stared up at the multitude of cocks Sharpied onto the stall's flimsy metal walls. He listened to the showers running, the clatter of voices on tile—*Molly is such a bitch, So hung-over right now, Did you fucking do it or not?*—receding, then swelling, then abruptly cut off.

"Marc?" Devin said.

He rubbed at the bruise on his chest, thinking how good it felt when, pinned to the bench, Devin lifted the bar for him and, suddenly, miraculously, he could breathe again.

◇◇◇

When Marcus first told Kara he was a non-practicing bisexual, she frowned, clicked her chopsticks at him, and said, no such thing. They'd been dating for nearly a year. They were studying and eating Chinese at his apartment in Ohio, which had essentially become her apartment, too. Evidenced by the bra on the bathroom floor, the soy milk in the fridge, the vase of slooping tulips on the bookcase.

"It's like saying you're an omnivore, but you don't eat meat," Kara said, slurping her noodles. "When really you mean you're just plain vegetarian."

He didn't know for sure why this upset him so much. Maybe it was because he'd been working up the nerve to tell her this for days—weeks!—and now she was treating it like it was no big deal.

"I'm telling you I'm attracted to men," he said.

"I know," Kara said. "And I'm telling you not to worry about it."

"It doesn't bother you that I'm attracted to men?"

"Does it bother you that I am?" Kara said.

Marcus laughed, then realized she wasn't joking. She was making a point. God, he loved her. She was so fucking brilliant. He'd never win an argument against her.

He should be relieved she didn't care. But the vegetarian metaphor still rankled him.

"It's not like that," he said. "It's more like . . . a priest is celibate, but it doesn't mean he's not a sexual being."

"I'm not saying you're asexual," Kara grinned. "Given what we just did an hour ago, I'd think that was obvious. I'm just saying, what's the difference? We're committed to each other no matter who we're attracted to."

"But I'm attracted to twice as many people as you," Marcus said. Lamely. Like it was a competition.

"Why are you making such a big deal about this?"

"Does it make me seem less masculine to you?"

"A lot of gay guys are *more* masculine than straight ones." Kara clicked her chopsticks at him again. "So no. If you want to know the truth, I think I already knew."

"How?"

"I don't know. I guess you have a way about you."

"Like a *gay* way? But you just said—"

"Yeah, I know. Can we just drop it? All I'm saying is, I don't think I could ever be with a guy who wasn't sensitive in the way you are. It's a compliment, really."

Marcus stared down at his orange chicken. He felt like there was more to say, but he didn't know what. Kara went back to her book on Tulipomania. Her PhD dissertation was on mass hysteria and took a sociohistorical approach. Documents on the seventeenth-century Dutch tulip craze were a primary source for her analysis. Marcus was getting a masters in poetry and was currently re-reading Frank O'Hara.

They were silent with their books and thoughts for the next half hour.

Kara looked up. "Is that why you always get so upset when they split the bill . . . ?"

"Yes!" Marcus said.

She was referring to how on dates, just the two of them, the waiters always split their bill without asking and Marcus (or Kara, if it was her turn) ended up paying for both anyway. This probably had nothing to do with Marcus and everything to do with the large herds of undergraduates who went out in their small college town and *always* split the bill, so it became an automatic assumption.

"They think I'm your gay best friend!" Marcus said.

"So?" Kara shrugged. "Aren't you?"

◇◇◇

"Do you ever wonder where you are on the Kinsey scale?" Marcus asked.

"What's that?" Devin said.

They were in the dorm room, Marcus sprawled out on his bed, reading a psychology book, Devin strumming his guitar to a Cat Stevens song. They were supposed to be studying for finals.

Marcus explained the scale: zero to six, with zero being exclusively heterosexual and six homosexual. He knew he could trust Devin to be open-minded and answer honestly, so he was surprised when he said, without hesitation, "Zero. Definitely zero."

Something had happened between them since that day at the gym. Marcus never worked out with Devin again, but they began eating dinner together and studied side by side at the library. When Dev came back from Spring Break and told Marcus he'd found out Savannah had been cheating on him (more out of being too lazy to break up with him than any malicious intent), Marcus knew he and Devin were officially friends.

"You know what she said?" Devin said. "She said, I assumed you were experimenting, too. I mean, it *is* college. Can you believe that?"

Marcus felt the phantom bruise on his chest—long healed—throb.

He assumed Devin would have a new girlfriend by the end of the week. Weirdly, he didn't. For all his popularity, Devin was strangely shy around girls. He confided in Marcus that Savannah had been his only experience. They'd dated since the sixth grade and never once broke up. He was depressed for a while, but this only solidified his friendship with Marcus. It became a nightly habit of theirs, before they fell asleep, to volley back and forth between their beds the names of girls they secretly liked—*Chloe Wright. Sarah Finny. Jamie Harding-Smith.*

The girls Marcus crushed on were often bookish, artistic types. Sometimes they carried cameras and took pictures of cigarette butts. Or had streaks of purple in their hair. Always they paled in comparison to how he felt about Devin.

Marcus barely knew any of the girls who belonged to the names Devin spoke with such reverence at night. When he looked them up online, he discovered Devin certainly had a type and it was conventionally beautiful in a Disney-princess way. Marcus could easily label these girls, based on hair color alone: Ariel. Belle. Cinderella.

Devin never actually made a move on any of these girls. They were interchangeable, more safely admired from a distance. That was, until a girl from his Bio class began hanging around their dorm room. Her name was Rachel Kennedy (she was a Belle, but a bit on the chubby side) and she had a mad crush on Devin. She showed up at all his wrestling matches, hung around the common room, waiting for Dev to emerge with his guitar, and knocked on their door to invite him to dinner every night.

"Could you tell her I'm not here?" Devin pleaded, and Marcus felt a perverse pleasure in lying to Rachel's face through the cracked door.

"You must really not like her," he said after she was gone.

"Too clingy," Devin said. But Marcus had a feeling it had more to do with her weight.

By the end of the semester, their friendship was undeniable. There was one final test:

"Any idea who you're gonna room with next year?" Marcus asked offhandedly one night, after they'd talked girls.

"Uh, duh," Devin said. "Did you have someone else in mind?"

"No," Marcus said. "Just checking."

"What about you?" Devin asked now, about the Kinsey scale. "Zero to six?"

How this question tormented Marcus! He had tried to convince himself he wanted to *be* Devin, that it was a crush of idolization—Dev's grades, his musical talent, his deft ability to navigate any social situation—but who was he kidding? Devin would walk in from the bathroom with just a towel around his waist and Marcus could feel his body temperature rise, and he'd know, deep down, that his crush was more than *intellectual*. He was attracted to more than Devin's *mind*. Reading the Kinsey study, Marcus longed to participate in a sexuality test that might determine once and for all his true attraction. He envisioned a *Clockwork Orange* type set-up, his eyelids clamped open, pornography—gay and straight—projected in front of him, an EKG machine reading the state of his arousal, assigning him a definitive number: Three. Four?

"Oh, yeah. Zero."

"I mean, how can you be half gay?" Devin said. "I thought it was an either/or."

"Yeah," Marcus said. He'd never hated himself more.

◇◇◇

The week leading up to his and Kara's final Newlywed session and Devin and Rachel's wedding tormented Marcus. The dove and the owl haunted him from the fridge. He was having diffi- culty filling out the required survey—Kara and he no longer did these together. It had basically become a chore. Every time he sat down to answer the questions, the answers that came to him dealt not with his marriage, but with Devin:

Q: Have you ever felt any jealousy toward another person your spouse has a close relationship with (i.e. co-worker, close friend, neighbor)? If so, please describe the nature of the situation.

A: Going to Devin's wrestling matches, watching him tumble on the mat with his opponent, gripping him in a headlock, then pinning him one, two, three.

Q: Do you or your spouse ever have difficulty sleeping in the same bed?

A: On their road trip to Boston to see Coldplay, sharing a hotel room, a queen bed, listening to him breathe in the dark, thinking: if I extended my leg and reached my foot out just a little . . .

Q: Have you and your spouse recently taken up any new hobbies?

A: That freak ice storm when they broke branches from the trees, marched across campus, hacking away at icicles, flinging snowballs at each other, how red his lips got.

Q: Have there been any new stresses on your relationship?

A: Walking in on them—Dev in his desk chair, Rachel on her knees.

"But you don't even like her," Marcus said later.
"Now I do."

Q: How often do you tell your spouse you love them?

A: Standing up at the wedding ceremony.

Oh god. Could he do that? No. Never. Devin was straight and getting married and Marcus *was* married and in love with Kara. It was absurd.

Then why did he keep seeing it? Dev in a suit at an altar, turning his head away from his bride to the audience, to where Marcus stood with something important to say.

He abandoned the survey and went to find Kara. She was at her desk, typing. He needed to tell her.

"Did you finish?" she said, about the survey.

"Are you in love with Liam?"

Kara looked up from her email. "Where'd that come from?"

"I don't know," Marcus said. "He's a good-looking guy. You see him at work everyday. I just thought. I mean, I wouldn't be mad."

"You know," Kara said, considering. "I never really thought about it."

"Come on."

"I'm serious. I mean, Liam's with Shellie and I'm with you."

"But that doesn't mean you're not attracted to him."

"Well, I'm not."

"Not even a little?"

"Seriously, Marcus? You think I'm cheating on you? Because I'm not. And I'm a little offended you'd think it."

That wasn't want he'd meant. It wasn't an accusation. He trusted Kara more than anyone. Sometimes he was scared of how much she loved him. He tried not to look at the tulip poem he'd written for their wedding, which she'd framed and hung over her desk.

"I'm sorry," he said. "It's just, don't you ever crush on anyone?"

"Sure," Kara said. "You."

How could she be so steadfast? Marcus had crushes all the time. The cute mailman told him to have a nice day and he was infatuated for a week. It wasn't fair.

"Is this about Rachel Kennedy?" Kara smirked.

"What? No!"

"I don't care who your crushes are," Kara said smugly. She turned back to her laptop. She'd thought she'd figured him out. "So long as at the end of the day, you're with me."

◇◇◇

Kara told him to meet her at the university at ten for their final Newlywed session. She'd gone to campus early to research in the library and Marcus was at home grading horribly redundant AP Lit papers on Kate Chopin's *The Awakening*. It was Saturday. The day of Devin's wedding. T-minus eleven hours.

He didn't know he was going to do it until he was in his car and he went straight through the light that was his turn to the university. Then he was taking the on-ramp to the interstate and he was heading north and he thought he was pretending. He was telling himself, I'll take the next exit and go back. Okay, the next. The next.

A half hour later his phone was buzzing and he shut it in the glove compartment. If he took Kara's call—or even checked a text—he knew he'd lose his nerve and would never make it to Kentucky. It was a ten-hour drive. No way was he going to make it to the ceremony, which was scheduled for seven. But if he only took two bathroom breaks, he'd arrive in plenty of time for the reception.

He was going to dance with Devin if it killed him. He was going to dance with the man he loved and say goodbye.

◇◇◇

He made it two hours away before having a panic attack, stopping, and calling his wife. His hands shook as he pressed the buttons.

"Marcus," Kara said. "Are you all right?"

"I thought I was in love with Devin," he said. Or tried to. He rubbed at his chest. He was having difficulty breathing. "But I don't think I am anymore."

"I know," Kara said. "Where are you?"

"At a rest stop in Georgia."

"The one outside Albany?"

"What? Yeah."

"Great. Don't move."

Twenty minutes later her Camry pulled up. She rolled down her window.

"Hey, handsome," she said. "Get in. Your suit's in the back."

Marcus shouldn't have been surprised. She always knew his mind before he did.

◇◇◇

The old man who sold them their tickets to the tulip garden informed them that only 15 percent of the flowers were still in bloom—15 percent and they still had to pay the exorbitant $40 entry fee, no refunds. Despite this warning, Marcus did not feel they had been adequately prepared for the disappointment that awaited them on the other side.

They swept through the dinky little turnstile, first she, then he, and out onto a brick path leading up to a white trellised archway. There was a dramatic bend after they crossed under this opening that revealed the entire garden from atop a minia-ture rise in the landscaping; it would have been quite a sight—it reminded him of the sensation Dorothy experienced upon arrival in Munchkinland, stepping out of the bleak tornado-displaced house and into a world of outrageous color—had they come but two weeks earlier. Instead, they were greeted by a not-unpleasant looking backyard: a weeping willow, a koi pond, beds of green. But, as they drew closer, the wreckage of the cold front that had drifted through Holland (Michigan—it was the closest he could get to the real thing) made itself known in the stalks of millions of poor denuded tulips, a few measly petals shriveling away on every hundredth flower.

As they loped down the path to the first empty bed—the red parrot tulip, according to the sign—the severity of his miscalcula-tion devastated him again and again. Everything—everything!—had been planned to a T: the hotel suite, the white suit coat, the sapphire ring in his pocket. They'd wandered the craft fair, lis-tened to banjo music, watched a performance of a traditional Dutch dance—children in caps and frills and wooden clogs—and all that was left was the tulips, the main event. But he hadn't thought to call ahead about the blooming. From the pictures on the Tulip Festival website, he'd assumed the timing of the week-end . . . but obviously the town couldn't control the weather.

Kara was making the best of it.

"There are still some with petals," she said, taking his hand. "Over here."

She knew, of course. He was standing in a tulip garden—or what *was* a tulip garden—wearing a white dinner jacket! They'd driven from their apartment in Ohio for five hours to see hun-dreds of varieties of her favorite flower. How could she *not* know?

As they strolled through the lipless fields, Marcus didn't know whether to laugh or cry. In his jacket pocket, he was clutch-ing the ring box in his fist. If he couldn't even get a proposal right, how could he a marriage? He stopped and Kara looked at him with concern.

He was telling himself that even the most beautiful things were flawed. How a ruined proposal made for a better story. He felt a poem forming somewhere.

"Don't," she said.

"What?"

"Don't you dare turn this into a metaphor," she said.

He smiled. "No, never."

"Promise?"

He promised.